TELL NO ONE

ALSO, BY DONNA M. ZADUNAJSKY

Novels
Broken Promises
Not Forgotten
The Accident

Books in Series
Family Secrets
Hidden Secrets
Twisted Secrets

Novellas
HELP ME!
Talk To Me

Young Adult Series
The Dead Girl Under the Bleachers
Buried Secrets
The Body in the Road

Young Adult
That Night

TELL NO ONE

by Donna M. Zadunajsky

TELL NO ONE

Copyright © 2024 by Donna M. Zadunajsky
All rights reserved. No part of this book may be reproduced or transmitted in any form or by any means, electronic or mechanical, including photocopying, recording, or by any information storage and retrieval system, without the written permission of the Publisher, except where permitted by law.

This novel is a work of fiction. Names, characters, places and incidents are either the product of the author's imagination or are used fictitiously. Any resemblance to actual persons, living or dead, events, or locales is entirely coincidental and not intended by the author.

ISBN:—Paperback- 979-8-3433-1650-6
ISBN:—Hardcover- 979-8-3304-5425-9

Book Cover Design by:
Interior Format by: Donna M. Zadunajsky
Editing by: Deborah Bowman Stevens

Connect with the Author:
http://www.donnazadunajsky.com
http://www.facebook.com/donnamzadunajsky
http://www.twitter.com/AuthorDonnaMZ
http://www.goodreads.com/donnamzadunajsky

Tayla
You are my inspiration...

Content Warning

This book contains
depictions of abuse
and self-harm.

Part One

*It only takes one second for your life to
change in ways that will change
who you are forever...*

Quote by Donna M. Zadunajsky

Judith
Now

One

Gripping the steering wheel, I leaned forward and peered out of the rain-splattered windshield. Sweat raced down the back of my neck. I hated driving in the rain, especially when it pours making it impossible to see the road.

Pain shot through my chest from the steering wheel digging into my ribs. Easing myself back, my shoulders tense, I sat perched in the leather seat. My eyes shifted to the dashboard, then back toward the street. I jerked the wheel, swerving into the other lane missing a parked car on the side of the road. A horn blared and I wrenched the steering wheel back to my side of the street.

"Dear, God, that was close," I mumbled, my heart hammering beneath my silk blouse. I hadn't seen the other car through the heavy blanket of rain.

Taking a deep breath in, I counted, one, two, three, then exhaled. My fingers were still wrapped tightly around the steering wheel, making the muscles in my forearms ache, afraid to let go. The storm had me on edge with warnings of tornadoes in the area. For a grown woman, I wasn't a big fan of thunderstorms. I hated the crackling and booming of thunder.

The hazy glow of yellow appeared in front of me before turning red. Slowing down, I approached the center of town which meant home was a few blocks away. I pressed on the brake, coming to a complete stop. Hands throbbing, I released them from the steering wheel and straightened each finger. I clenched my hand into a fist then released. Blood circulated through each finger. The numbness and tingling disappearing.

Sweat zig-zagged down the back of my neck. Another bead of sweat formed along the hairline above my forehead. The temperature in the vehicle had risen a few degrees since leaving the office. Pressing the AC button, cool air began to blow out from the vents. I let out a sigh of relief, my muscles wilting beneath my shirt. Thunder rumbled in the distance then a bolt of lightning shot across the sky.

A person, their features blurred by the rain, ran in front of my car, holding an umbrella. I turned and peered out the driver's side window. Heavy rainfall flooded the streets, filling the sewers. The person stepped into a large puddle, soaking their shoes before skittering down the sidewalk looking for shelter.

Fifteen minutes later, I arrived in front of my home. I stared out the windshield, the wipers thrashing back and forth as I watched the garage door rise. To my surprise, my husband Scott's car wasn't there, which meant he could be stuck out in the storm. Although he worked further away than I did, he had also left work before me. Closing my eyes, I whispered, "Please Lord keep him safe."

Once inside the garage, I turned off the ignition, but didn't get out of the car. I sat back against the seat and closed my eyes, letting the stress of the drive home roll off me. My mouth began to water as I imagined the glass of red wine I was going to pour myself once I got inside the house. But right this minute, I needed to take a second to calm my nerves.

A deep breath in, then out...

I slowly opened my eyes, catching a movement in the rearview mirror. My hand grasped the handle of the driver's side door and swung it open. The wind had blown our garbage can across the driveway and into the yard.

This just wasn't my day.

Rain pelted my body at all angles as I ran to retrieve the can, dragging it back inside the garage. I closed the garage door and stepped inside the house. Removing my rain-soaked designer blazer, I hung it in the laundry room, strolled into the kitchen, and placed my purse on the chair. The house sat quiet, except for the occasional gust of wind and rain smacking against the house and roof.

It didn't seem like anyone was home. Was my daughter Mia out with her boyfriend Trevor? I glanced at the clock on the wall which read 5:58 p.m. It was possible, she usually stayed at the school when he had football practice. Though I doubted they were practicing in this storm. Unless they were caught in it too. Thoughts ran wild in my head, praying they were okay. I grabbed my cell phone from my purse and dialed Mia's number, but it went straight to voicemail. Strange, Mia's phone was never turned off. It wasn't the cell towers because my phone still worked.

My body tense, I poured myself a glass of wine. I swallowed, my throat parched; I lifted the glass to my lips and drank down half. After pouring more into the glass, I then headed for the stairs to get out of these wet clothes and to take a hot shower. I removed my three-inch heels, letting the straps hang from my index finger before climbing the stairs.

The floorboards creaked and moaned as I climbed the stairs to the second floor. Stopping at the top, I glanced at the two closed doors to my left: the furthest being Mia's bedroom. My son Ethan had left for college two weeks ago. I didn't hear anything but the storm outside, which meant that no one was home but me.

Once in my bedroom, I closed the door and walked into the bathroom. The hot steaming shower caressed my body, relaxing my muscles. The stress of the day went washing down the drain. It felt good to be home.

Minutes later, dressed in comfy clothes, I left the bedroom. I stood at the top of the stairs, staring down the hall at Mia's bedroom door again. I wasn't sure what was bothering me. Positive that no one was home, but something stirred inside me. My motherly instincts setting in, making me feel like something was wrong.

I positioned my foot on the first step and stopped. A soft *banging* came from down the hall near Mia's bedroom. I had told

Scott several times that the pipes were making noises and needed to be looked at. I grabbed the banister, turned, and made my way down the hall toward Mia's bedroom, flicking on the hall lights as I went.

Placing my ear against the door, I listened. Mia didn't like it when I came into her room unannounced. A fight I grudgingly lost multiple times. I hated fighting with her, so I agreed to give her some space. Some independence.

Being a mother was hard, especially these days when disciplining your child was frowned upon. Not that I ever hit my children.

There it was again but not as subtle as before.

"Mia," I whispered, tapping a knuckle against the door. "Are you home?"

Nothing.

Thunder boomed, rattling the windows all around me.

I jumped at the sharp crack of lightning, then the lights went out, leaving me in darkness.

"Shit!" I blinked several times, waiting for my eyes to adjust. My cell phone. Where was my phone? Patting my pockets, I felt the hard case. I pulled the phone out and tapped the flashlight icon. Light illuminated.

Placing my hand on the doorknob, I turned, and found it locked. I stretched my arm above my head, sliding my fingers along the frame until I felt the key. It was something Scott and I agreed to do for emergencies if we needed to get inside the room.

Just in case the kids forgot that they had locked the door before falling asleep. Even though as their parents we had protested against the door being locked in the first place. I was once a teenager too and wanted nothing more than my space from my parents. But still, we frowned upon the door being locked. Though, if Scott were the one knocking, Mia wouldn't hesitate to let her dad inside.

I hesitated, gripping the key in my hand. Once I opened the door there was no turning back. I wasn't in the mood to fight with Mia which we seemed to do constantly since we had gotten back from our family trip to the Bahamas. I tried to get her to talk to me several times when we were on vacation and after we arrived back home, but she wouldn't have anything to do with me. Wouldn't even let me in her room. I thought maybe her, and Trevor had broken up, and she just wanted to hide in her room with her heartache. But that thought defused when he came to pick her up to go to the mall that next day.

The key slipped from my shaky hand and onto the floor. Kneeling, I grasped the key between my fingers and placed it into the lock. I closed my eyes and swallowed, waiting for the *click* as I turned the key to the right. "You're not doing anything wrong," I whispered to myself. "You're just checking to see if she's home, oh and to check the pipes for leakage."

The hinges squeaked, echoing through the upstairs hall as I pushed the door open. My eyes drifted around the room, landing on the pink duvet I had bought her when she was seven which lay across the bed with a dark pink throw on the end. The pillows on her bed were upright and fluffed. *Mia was good at making her bed and keeping her room clean compared to Ethan,* my mind noted.

My eyes scanned the room, focusing on the desk in the corner which sat vacant. Mia wasn't here. I moved around the room, stopping by the window overlooking the street below. The clouds moved quickly by, and the rain ceased, leaving the ground saturated and the streets flooded. A burst of light shot across the sky, making me jump again. I let out a small laugh, allowing my shoulders to sink beneath my T-shirt. "It's just the storm, Judith. Chill out." Truth was, I hated everything about storms. I feared the darkness, especially when the power went out. Consequently, due to my childhood.

Using the flashlight to guide my way, I moved toward the closet and peeked inside. My hand automatically went for the light switch, forgetting for a second that the electricity had gone out.

I scanned the closet. Stuffed teddy bears lined the shelf along the ceiling. Shoes laid in a heap near the back corner and clothes hung haphazardly off the hangers. My OCD taking charge, I stepped inside and began straightening her clothes. Neat and tidy just the way I liked it.

Plop, plop.

My ears perked. The sound came from the other side of the wall. *Or in the wall.* Could it be the pipes? Were they leaking?

"Just great," I muttered. "Where was Scott when I needed him?" I was always making things out to be more than they were; something my husband constantly expressed to me.

I walked out of the closet and stood outside the closed bathroom door. Like before, I placed my hand on the knob. Was Mia home after all? I didn't hear the shower running. No sound of Mia moving around on the other side of the door, recalling that she usually played music when she took a bath or a shower.

My stomach twisted into a knot, dreading a fight with Mia for intruding on her privacy. Call it mother's intuition, but something didn't feel right.

I turned the knob, finding it unlocked, and pushed the door open.

My legs buckled and I dropped to my knees onto the tiled floor.

Two

My scream ricocheted off the walls, vibrating back into my ears like a boomerang. I crawled to the tub. My hands and knees were now saturated in blood.

Mia's blood.

Water splashed out of the tub as I pulled her toward me, clutching her body into mine. Her eyes fluttered open then closed when I looked at her face.

She was still alive.

Still breathing.

"Oh, Mia," I muttered. My heart swelled with relief but at the same time I was horrified at what she'd done. Why? Why would she do this? Suicide?

Tears poured from my eyes. I cradled her in my arms, rocking her like a newborn baby. I let out another horrifying scream; one that I was sure could be heard from miles away. Then as if someone had slapped me across the face, I spun away from the tub still holding onto her.

Afraid to let go.

Afraid I will lose her.

Afraid of everything I'd come to love so deeply would fade away.

My eyes searched helplessly for something, anything, I could place over the cut on her wrist. My fingers slipped from the knob on the cabinet, wet with her blood. I rummaged through the items cluttered under the sink, tossing them aside. Something cloth-like touched my fingers. Peering into the cabinet, I spotted a box of overnight maxi pads, extra-long. I yanked the box out, knocking everything in the way onto the floor and placed it between my thighs. I plunged my hand inside the open box and pulled out a pad. With my teeth, I peeled the paper back, revealing the sticky tape on one side. I pressed the pad against the cut and wrapped it around her wrist.

My eyes shifted to the water in the tub, growing pinker by the second. Reaching across her body, I lifted her other arm. Blood ran from the open wound.

My breath caught in my throat. More tears spilled from my eyes.

I dragged her weightless body out of the tub, her bony hips poking into me. I hadn't known she had lost so much weight. She looked nothing like she did on our family vacation last month. I cradled her in my lap like I did when she was a baby and wrapped her other wrist.

Help…

I needed to call for help. My cell phone. Where was my phone? I had it in my hand when I opened the door. It must have fallen somewhere in her room.

Letting out another ear-piercing scream as if my life depended on it. Mia's life did depend on it!

"Please, Mia, don't you dare die on me," I bawled.

A door slammed shut. My husband was home. *Oh, thank God.*

"Help!" I shouted, again. "Scott up here. Please help!"

Footfalls pounded up the stairs.

"Please, help!" I screamed from the top of my lungs, my body shaking. My throat was raw. More tears leaked from my eyes.

Heavy footsteps hit the wood floor, racing toward Mia's room. Then he appeared in the doorway.

Three

It wasn't Scott, but our neighbor, Dave Palmer standing in the entryway of Mia's bathroom. His eyes wide with horror. He stumbled back, his leg bumping the bed post and placed a hand to his mouth. "Dear God. Oh, my…" he stammered, taking in the sight.

"Help!" I cried out. "Call for help!"

As if a switch had been flicked on, he gave me a curt nod, changing from a horrified friend, neighbor, and parent to a person of authority. Dave pulled his cell phone from the back pocket of his jeans and dialed a number which I assumed was 9-1-1.

"Yes, I need an ambulance at 2821 Gabbles Street. Yes, my neighbor Mia Barnes. Of course, yes, she has deep cuts on her wrists. Bleeding…" he paused, swallowing. "A pulse?"

His eyes darted from the floor to my face. I nodded.

"Yes, she still has a pulse."

My ears perked to the sound of sirens heading toward my home. I was so thankful that the fire station was less than a mile down the street. My eyes dropped to the floor next to Dave's leg. His golden retriever had climbed the stairs, following her owner. The dog sat next to him, staring at me and whimpered. *Could the dog sense that something was wrong?* Dave's hand went to his side, and he stroked the dog's head. The dog leaned into him, glancing up at her owner.

"They're here," he said, shoving his phone back into his pocket.

I nodded, hugging my daughter into me, not wanting to let her go.

I couldn't let her go.

I was afraid to let her go.

"Please, baby, don't you dare die on me," I whispered in her ear.

"Up here," Dave shouted, stepping into the hall, out of eyesight.

"They're here Mia. Please hold on, baby." Her eyes fluttered open then closed.

Mumbled voices floated down the hall; then two paramedics appeared in the doorway. Unlike Dave, neither paramedic grimaced at the sight of my daughter lying in a pool of her own blood.

"Ma'am, you'll need to let us check her," one of the paramedics said.

I stifled a cry but didn't move. I didn't want to let go of her.

"Judith," Dave said from behind them. "Let them help her."

I looked at Mia in my arms, feeling the weight of their eyes on me. She was so fragile I was afraid she'd break into pieces if I let go of her.

"Ma'am."

I laid her head down on the bathroom floor, scooched to the side, and pushed myself up. My foot slipped and I nearly fell on top of her. The young paramedic grabbed my arm, pulling me toward him and away from Mia. I stumbled into the bedroom, my legs rubbery, and collapsed into Dave's arms. He pulled me in tight, shushing me as if I were a child having a nightmare.

I cried harder.

"Okay, she's stable. Let's get her on the stretcher."

I pulled away and watched them carry her out of the bedroom and down the stairs. They placed her inside the back of the ambulance vehicle. I climbed inside. The doors closed just as Scott pulled up behind us.

Four

The thought of not telling Scott myself tore at my heartstrings. Dave would fill him in, and he'd be at the hospital after we arrived. My body jolted forward as the ambulance sped away. With one hand holding onto Mia's hand, the other hand grabbed the corner of the bench to keep myself from falling.

Once we arrived and went inside, the staff swarmed around Mia. They quickly wheeled her down the hall and into a curtained room, I wanted to go with her, but another nurse held me back. I stood in the emergency area feeling numb, alone, and broken. I knew they had to check her wrists and stitch her up; make sure she hadn't lost too much blood, even though I already knew she had.

A cold, soft touch brushed against my skin. I turned to see a young woman wearing dark blue scrubs. Her eyebrows were drawn together, her head tilted.

"Ma'am," she said in a hushed whisper.

My mouth opened but nothing came out. This was the first time I had nothing to say. If Mia was here beside me, she would make a comment about me being too quiet. I'm the talker when I'm around people. Not that I always have something to say. I just like conversation; unlike my job where I only listen to people talk.

The young woman's eyes dropped down. I followed her gaze. My blood-soaked shirt and pants had her attention.

"It's not mine," I replied.

She nodded. "I know. Please come with me."

Like an obedient dog, I followed her down the hall and into a room. It wasn't a room where Mia was being helped, but a small room with a couple of chairs, a bed, and a restroom.

"Here, you can put these on if you want." She handed me a bluish-gray T-shirt with the hospital logo on the front, Willow Memorial Hospital, and matching sweatpants.

The skin on my face felt tight, like it would break if I tried to smile.

"You can stay in here. I will come and get you when the doctor is finished," she stated.

Before I could answer, she left the room, closing the door behind her. Now I was alone in a room I didn't want to be in, but I also didn't want to be out there where people might see me. Where someone would recognize me. I'm thankful we're out of town and away from people we know but they would still come to this hospital as it was the closest one around. Our neighbors would talk about what Mia did. Although a part of me doesn't care what they will say. I just want her to be okay. I want her to be alive.

Like a snail, I moved in slow motion toward a door across from me with a silver metal plate labeled restroom. Once inside, I closed the door and a light automatically flicked on. I'm focused on the mirror in front of me. Not sure who I'm looking at anymore. The shirt I'm wearing was saturated in blood, along with my sweatpants. I pulled the bloody shirt over my head and stared at my skin stained with her blood.

Mia's blood.

My baby girl.

Tears slid down my face. I don't wipe them away. Why should I? I deserve this pain that courses through my body like a raging river. My fingers brushed against my skin like I'm finger-painting. The blood was now dry.

I stepped toward the sink and twisted the handle. The clear water turned pink as I washed the blood from my hands. With a vigorous force I began to scrub my skin with the soap mounted on the wall. Pink water splashed in all directions, staining the white porcelain sink, but I didn't care. I only wanted to get the blood off my skin like it was poison.

I took the bloody shirt I pulled off me and ran it under the cold water. Twisting and wringing until the water runs clear. I take the soaking wet shirt and wring it twice more before turning on the hot water and using it as a rag to wipe the skin of my belly and chest. I rinsed and repeated until I had wiped away most of the blood before tossing it in the garbage can. I don't need it, nor do I want it. The memory alone will forever be cemented into my brain.

Tugging the clean shirt over my head, I looked down at my pants. I slithered out of them one leg at a time, careful not to fall. My legs were still weak and shaky. When I finished, my eyes scanned over the mess I had made. Ripping paper towels from the dispenser, I wiped the sink clean. No Mia blood anywhere when I finished. No one needed to see what I did. The mess I had made. Though I wasn't thinking about the blood anymore but all the years I had shielded love and affection away from Mia. No matter how hard I tried, I'm ashamed that I became my mother. A person I never wanted to be. A heartless bitch. She was a woman with no backbone. A woman who should have protected her daughter from her abusive husband, my father. No, instead she stood like a coward in the corner allowing him to beat us both and then lock me into the hall closet with no food or water for days.

The tears were now gone, only to be replaced by anger. These were emotional steps I knew all too well. The same ones I repeated constantly to all my patients.

I finished cleaning up and opened the door. My body stiffened at the site of Scott standing in front of me. His face was red and puffy. Had he been crying too?

"Scott," I whimpered.

He opened his arms and I fell into him. The tears I had wiped away returned.

Five

We sat in the room with walls painted a smoky gray. A color I would have never chosen as it signified grief. Which seemed to fit my life right now.

I told him everything that had happened when I had arrived home from work. The moments leading up to finding Mia in her bathroom in the tub, and all that blood.

"That's when Dave appeared in the doorway and called 9-1-1," I sobbed.

Scott pulled me into his arms and held me close. His heartbeat pulsed in my ear, fast then slow. I couldn't do this without him.

He was my savior.

He kept me grounded.

We had completed one another since the day we had met.

I pulled away and wiped the salty tears from my face with my fingers. He held out a few Kleenexes and I dabbed my eyes, then blew my nose. Exhaustion swept through me; no doubt from everything that had happened since I'd arrived home from work.

"What time is it?" I asked, scanning the room for a clock but not finding one.

Scott peered down at his wrist. "Almost nine."

Nine? My God, what was happening with my little girl? My thoughts were running wild. "It's been hours. Why hasn't anyone come to talk to us? You don't think…"

Scott placed a hand on each side of my face, looking into my eyes. "Breathe. Don't think that way. Mia is fine. I can feel it," he said, then kissed my forehead.

My eyes on his, I took in a deep breath, held it, then released it. My body sank into the chair like quicksand. *I had to hold on for her. I had to be strong for my Mia.*

My ears perked and I whipped my head toward the door when it opened and a nurse wearing Mickey Mouse scrubs stood in the doorway. "Mr. and Mrs. Barnes?"

Without thinking, I jumped to my feet, unaware of how wobbly my legs were. Scott stood and stepped behind me, placing an arm around my midsection to keep me from falling over. He was good at reading me. We were good together. There was no way I could face this without him.

"Mia?" I questioned.

"She's stable. Would you like to go see her?" the nurse asked.

My head bobbed up and down like a bobblehead.

Scott guided me out of the room and down the hall toward the elevator. My eyes darted in all directions, looking at the faces as we followed the nurse. *I wondered if they knew why I was here. Did they know about Mia? That my Mia tried to…to end her life? Did they think I was a bad mother?* I sucked in a breath, then another one until I had to stop in the middle of the busy hallway flooded with nurses and doctors. I swayed, my head feeling woozy. My knees began to buckle, and I felt myself falling to the floor, my legs slipping out from under my feet. *Was I having an anxiety attack?*

"Hey, you're all right," Scott said, enveloping me in his arms.

Lifting my head, I stared into his eyes. His words were seeping slowly into my ear. My brain was fogged by sadness and fear of losing my little girl. I couldn't lose her. Didn't she know that? Did she know I loved her with every ounce of my heart, my soul?

"Let's get her a wheelchair," the nurse said.

Scott held me tight until the nurse rolled the wheelchair to me, and I sat down. With my head down, Scott steered me toward the elevators away from wandering eyes. The scratched and fingerprinted silver metal doors slid open, we all climbed inside, and the nurse tapped the button for the fifth floor.

The fifth floor was the psychiatric ward. I only knew this because one of the other psychiatrists where I worked just told me that they had to send a patient there because they tried to harm themselves.

A rush of warmness flowed through my body and my heart raced with anticipation, dizziness still swirling in my head. They were going to commit Mia to the psychiatric ward. No, they had already committed her. Once a person did what she did, it was mandatory to place the patient in an in-care facility. She would then have to go to counseling. She would have to talk about why she did what she did. God, I couldn't even say the words. Part of me felt jealous that the doctors would know before I did.

The elevator jolted to a stop and the doors swished open. Bleeps and pings of diagnostic equipment filled my ears. The nurse stepped out and Scott pushed me behind her. It hadn't occurred to me until now that I was being selfish. My husband was holding it together because of me, but he had always been good at doing that. He had always been the strong one in our marriage. Though that still didn't make it right. He had to be hurting too. Mia and her dad had always been close. Something I had always been jealous of. When Mia was little, I would take her places, like the nail salon and the library. A girl's day. Now that she was older, we didn't do mother-daughter things together. Something I missed desperately. But that was my fault. I'm the one to blame for making my work, my job, come first before her, before my family.

The nurse scanned her ID card on a small, square, black keypad. The door unlocked with a *click*.

Six

The small, narrow hall seemed to go on forever, but was only twenty feet long. It's funny how our minds can envision something that isn't there. The stress was overpowering our minds to the point that we started imagining things. Especially the things we see every day. The things we take for granted, like my daughter.

My eyes were focused on the wall, a pastel green, going in and out like a camera lens, blurry then clear. Turning my head, I saw a small bathroom to my right. Back in front of me, the room was wide open. The fluorescent lights hummed above me as Scott moved forward, the bed now coming into view. Mia lay sleeping in the bed. She looked so fragile underneath the white sheet and thin blanket the nurses had placed upon her. For a moment, I wondered if she was cold. Mia loved having mounds of blankets on top of her when she was in her bed at home or cuddled up on the sofa in the living room. I would make a mental note to bring in one of her favorite blankets.

My eyes dropped to her arms lying beside her body on top of the blanket, each wrapped in white gauze. I choked back a sob. Scott squeezed my shoulder. I slipped from his touch, stood, and hurried to her bedside, wanting nothing more than to be near her. I wanted it to be me she saw first when she opened her eyes. She needed to know she wasn't alone. That I was here for her. That I have always been here for her. That I loved her, and I would take care of her.

"The doctor will be in to talk to you both soon," the nurse said before turning and leaving. The door clicked shut behind her.

I nodded at her words but kept my eyes on Mia. Scott moved and stood on the other side of the bed. His fingers trailed up and down Mia's arm in a soothing motion. Something he had done when she was a baby as he held her in his arms. He was the greatest father to our kids, and he was being so strong, but he didn't have to be. I wouldn't hold it against him if he cried. Men cried all the time in my office. They were just as human as anyone else.

I reached behind me and pulled the wooden chair closer to the bed and sat, carefully sliding my hand under hers. Her hand was cold. When she was little, Mia hated her hands being cold. I placed my other hand on top to help warm her skin without applying too much pressure. I didn't want to cause her any pain. Was she in pain? Clearly, she was, but not the kind I was referring. No one would try to commit suicide if they weren't hurting inside. What could've happened that would make her want to die?

My eyes moved from the bandage on her wrist to her face. She looked at peace. *God, what was wrong with me? She wasn't dead. You only said things like that when someone was dead and lying in a casket.*

A tear leaked out from the corner of my eye, leaving a single streak down my face. I licked my lips, tasting the salty tear. Another tear dropped from my chin, blotting the white sheet. I needed to stop this and be strong for Mia. She couldn't wake up and find me sobbing like a baby beside her. I was her mother. I had to be the tough one and let her know that we would get past this. That we would get her whatever help she needed.

The door to the room opened. I glanced over my shoulder to see a spindly man wearing a white doctor's coat. He wore dark, rimmed glasses, and had a five o'clock shadow. He stopped at the edge of the bed, a chart in his hand.

"Hi, I'm Dr. Ron DuSol. I will be Mia's attending doctor during her stay."

Scott and I both nodded simultaneously.

"Mia's in stable condition, but I'm admitting her in the inpatient care program for at least three weeks. This way she can get the help that she needs, and we can evaluate her depression," Dr. DuSol said, as he looked from Scott to me.

"Mia's not depressed," I quipped.

"People with depression can easily hide it from the people they love. It's not uncommon for loved ones to be surprised by this as you are," Dr. DuSol stated. "I have her on a low dose of Tramadol for the pain and will start her on Zoloft in a day or two. I'll monitor her progress and increase her meds as needed."

"What do we need to do?" Scott asked. "Can we stay with her?"

"I'm afraid family can't visit while she's in the inpatient care program. She'll have several group sessions with other teens her age that are going through what she is dealing with and one-on-one sessions with me and a psychiatrist," Dr. DuSol replied.

My head bobbed up and down, letting the words register. *Mia would be all alone. I wouldn't be able to be here with her. She'd think I have abandoned her, like my mother did me. That I wasn't here for her. But I'm here now, wasn't that what matter?*

Seven

As the days went by, I kept my schedule full at work and myself busy at home with cleaning and organizing. My mind needed to be occupied with other things, not that I ever stopped thinking and worrying about Mia. She was all alone in that hospital. Well, not totally alone, but she had no family there. For whatever reason, we weren't allowed to visit during the three weeks. I had had patients in the psych ward before and they were permitted to have family visits. Then it clicked in my head.

Mia didn't want me there.

She didn't want me to visit her.

Was she ashamed of me?

Had Scott gone to see her?

He would have told me, wouldn't he?

My mind whirled as I moved around the house.

My slippers scuffed against the wood steps as I climbed the stairs to the second floor. Instead of heading to my bedroom, I walked down the hall and stopped in front of the last door on the right, Mia's room. I hadn't been in here since that awful night I had found her, just two days ago. Scott said he had cleaned everything up, so I didn't have to see it. What would I do without him? Had it been hard for him to be in this room? To clean up his daughter's blood? I hadn't asked him. I thought only about Mia and myself.

My hand hovered over the metal knob, but I couldn't find it in myself to turn it and go inside. It would be wrong for me to go into her room without her here, wouldn't it? But what if I searched her room and found evidence as to why she did what she did?

Would she be angry with me for snooping?

Was it wrong for me to want to know the real reason?

Should I stay out of her business?

Should I give her space? And if so, how much space?

I had done nothing but give her space. If I had been in my daughter's life before what had happened, maybe she wouldn't have attempted suicide?

The images of that evening flashed in my brain. I could still picture the way my daughter's eyes were clouded over, but no drugs had been found in her system. But then again, she had lost a significant amount of blood which would cause her body to become weak and unresponsive.

What was wrong with me? I needed to keep it together. I was stronger than I was acting at this very moment. Inside I was cracking like glass. Truth was, I needed answers. I needed to know why she did it, but instead I turned and walked down the hall only to stop halfway.

The door to Ethan's room was ajar. I hadn't known he was home or had Scott gone into his room and forgot to close the door? Before I could stop myself, I reached out and pushed on the door. The hinges squeaked before bouncing off the door stop. I placed one foot in front of the other and entered his bedroom.

Clothes were strewn around the room. I was sure when he had left for college it was clean. But how would I know? I hadn't been in his room for at least a week. Right before my daughter tried to take her own life.

I moved forward, flipping on the light switch. A narrow-unmade bed sat in front of me, which told me he had slept here, but when? Had he been home for a while now without me knowing? No, I was sure he hadn't been here before today. I would know, right?

I would have felt him in this house.

I would have seen him.

Didn't all mothers feel something when their children were around? When something happened to them? Like when I had a bad feeling and went into Mia's room and found her in the bathtub? Had I been so unconnected with my children that I didn't know what was happening in their lives? Was I that bad of a mother?

Stepping further into the room, my fingers glided along the wall, feeling the rough texture of the paint on my fingertips. My fingers grazed over the books on the bookshelf, feeling the foiled coarseness that bonded the books together.

I stopped when I came to his desk. Weird how it was cleaner than the rest of the room. No papers or books lying on top. He was never one to sit and do his homework at home, but he always seemed to get straight A's in all his classes.

I couldn't stop myself and opened the top drawer of the desk. Pens and pencils laid scattered about. Nothing else. I closed the drawer and opened another one. Crumbled paper sat inside. Reaching in, I grabbed one and unwrinkled it. It was an old math paper. I tossed it into the garbage can next to the desk and seized another one. This one appeared to have indentations where words had been written. I had never been a nosy parent when it came to my children. Strict maybe, but never nosy. I should have been more involved in their life. Been a mother who listened instead of shouted orders. A friend to my kids.

"What the fuck are you doing in my room!"

A flush of adrenaline tingled through my body. My head whipped around, and I shoved the paper I had in my hand into the front pocket of my dress pants. "Ethan."

"I asked you a fucking question?"

"I...I was just cleaning up," I sputtered. *Why was I stuttering?* But mostly, when had I become afraid of my own son? He startled me because I hadn't known he was home. He was supposed to be at college. Why was he home? Had Scott called him and told him about Mia? I bent over and picked up a T-shirt, then another one.

"Leave it!"

My face flushed and sweat materialized along my hairline then raced down my spine, stopping at the strap of my bra. The air in the room seemed to rise a few hundred degrees. Without hesitation I dropped the shirts where I stood and quickly moved toward the door. I needed to get out of his room. But I couldn't get out. Ethan was blocking the doorway. I drew in a breath and stood taller. More sweat slid down my back.

I lifted my head until our eyes met. Ethan was taller than me by seven inches. He stared down at me before stepping aside. I crossed the threshold, now standing in the hall. I turned toward the door just as he slammed it in my face, making me jump backward. I drew in a breath and exhaled. My knees began to buckle, nearly collapsing where I stood. *Why was he home? But more importantly, why was he acting this way? Why was he so angry?*

I turned and quickly scurried down the stairs to the kitchen. I grabbed a glass, filled it with water and gulped it down. My hand slipped into the pocket of my pants and pulled out the paper I had taken from Ethan's room. I unfolded the balled-up paper, pressing out the creases. You could see the indentation where there were words written. I smoothed out the paper and grabbed a pencil from the drawer beside me. Carefully I rubbed the pencil lead across the paper. Words began to appear. When I finished, I set the pencil on the counter and read what was written on the paper.

Eight

My stomach dropped and a swirl of dizziness swam in my head. I grabbed the counter with one hand to keep myself from falling to the floor. Why did Ethan have a note written to whom I wasn't sure? And what did it mean?

I looked down at the paper in my hand, trying to steady the shakes as I read the words once again.

Do you think killing yourself is a way out? That you can escape me? You'll never get away from me. You're a smart girl. I know I can count on you to keep my secret. Our secret. Do you think you can just end your life because of this? I won't make it that easy for you. I need you. You need me. So, don't think about trying it again!

There was no mistake about it. The handwriting did belong to my son. I was sure of it. My eyes scanned the words again and again. Should I confront him about this? Or should I wait and search his room after he leaves for school on Sunday.

"What are you reading?"

I jumped and the letter fluttered to the floor. I twirled around to see Ethan standing in the doorway. Dropping to my knees, I scooped up the paper between my fingers and folded it into a small square, shoving it back into my pocket.

"Nothing. It's nothing," I replied, my heart palpitating.

He stared at me quizzically. "Okay, if you say so. I'm heading out to meet the guys."

"I didn't know you were home this weekend," I asked, swallowing the lump lodged in my throat.

"Yeah, I wanted to hang out with the guys. You have a problem with that?"

I flinched, hurt by his words. *What was going on with my son? Why was he using that tone with me?* my mind whirled with questions. Standing there, I waited for him to leave, listening for the front door to close before my knees buckled and I sank to the floor. My body trembled with fear. I had never seen my son like this. With the way Ethan was acting, it slipped my mind to ask him if he knew about his sister. I hadn't even thought about calling him to tell her. Had Scott called him? I would have to ask him later. Ethan did say he was home to hang with the guys. He had never mentioned Mia. What I did know was that there was something going on with my son and I needed to find out what.

"Judith, you need to get up and go upstairs," a voice said inside my head.

Lifting myself up off the floor, I walked out of the kitchen and up the stairs. I stood in front of Ethan's bedroom door, reaching my hand out, I touched the cold metal knob and turned.

I shouldn't have been surprised to find the door locked. Straightening my arm up above my head, I ran my fingers along the trim above the door for the key, but found nothing. Again, I shouldn't have been shocked; of course, my son would take the key. Which also meant, he had something to hide.

I hurried down the hall and reached above Mia's bedroom door. Her key was gone too. "Son of a bitch," I muttered. *The key was there two days ago when I had gone into Mia's bedroom,* shaking the thought from my head, I turned and raced to my bedroom and into the bathroom. I yanked the drawer open and rummaged through the drawer for a bobby pin. Once I found one, I sprinted out of the room.

A *click* and the knob turned.

Pushing the door open, I flicked on the light. I started with the bookshelf, fanning through the few books Ethan owned, but found nothing.

My eyes skimmed over the desk before I opened the top drawer. Like before, there were crumbled pieces of paper inside. I grabbed one and unfolded it. Once again, there was nothing left inside. I moved onto the drawer beneath it. After not finding anything else in the desk, I walked around the room until I stood in front of the nightstand beside the bed. On top there was a magazine, two empty glasses, which I had mentioned multiple times to them to take their dirty dishes back to the kitchen when they were done, which never seemed to get through their heads.

There were three drawers.

My fingers curled around the brass knob of the top drawer. The wood scraped against the side as I opened it, finding it filled with protein wrappers. I picked through the garbage, but nothing popped out. I closed the drawer and opened the second one. My knees buckled and I stumbled back, tripping over the pile of clothes on the floor, landing with a hard *thud*.

Nine

My tailbone ached. I was sure there would be a bruise there later. I climbed to my knees and rubbed my hand over my tailbone. The pain slowly subsided. I crawled to the open drawer. Reaching a hand inside, I pulled out several photos. Why would Ethan have polaroids of girls? And not just normal candid photos that people took of other people but ones that were inappropriate.

I shuffled through the small stack feeling even more uneasy by the second. Ethan had taken naked pictures of random girls. Dropping onto the mattress, I brought the photos closer to my eyes. My heart was pounding like a racehorse. I thought for sure I was about to have a heart attack. I swallowed, but still felt the liquid making its way up into my throat. If you weren't looking for it, you would miss the tears running down the girl's face. How long had he been doing this? Horrified by what I was seeing, I knew I had to do something, but what? Should I show these to Scott? Ethan would know if I took the photos. That someone was in his room. Would he know it was me? He had caught me in here earlier. But why should I care what he thinks? These were naked pictures of girls!

I had to think because I wasn't sure what I was going to do about this. I laid the photos out on the bed, my stomach sour with disgust. Digging my cell phone out from the pocket of my pants, I opened the camera app and took several pictures. This way if my son destroyed them, I at least had a copy.

Then it occurred to me. What the hell was I thinking? I gathered the pictures, scooping them up in my hand and sat back down on the edge of the mattress, my eyes scanning the girl's body. I couldn't let him keep doing this, keep taking these pictures, destroying other young girls' lives. What mother would allow her son to keep doing something so…so disturbing and horrible? I thought I was going to be sick and puke! My son is a monster.

"Come on, Judith," I muttered. "You're trained for things like this. What would you tell your patients?"

I sat thinking for a long time, occasionally glimpsing down at the photos. I swallowed as a sour taste entered my mouth, again. Ethan may be my son, and I may be intruding on his privacy, but this is my house and there was no way in hell I was letting him keep these pictures, but how do I stop him from taking more pictures and hurting more young girls?

I leaned forward and pulled the drawer all the way open. Rooting through the remaining items, I didn't find anything else except the key for the bedroom door and snatched it up. I closed the drawer and opened the third drawer. There was nothing inside but magazines. I closed them and hurried around the bed to the other side. I did the same thing. I searched through all three drawers, thankfully finding nothing else.

Leaving Ethan's bedroom, I locked and closed the door behind me. I scurried down the hall and replaced the key above Mia's door. Hesitating, I turned the knob and went inside her room. It looked so empty without her in it.

I closed the door behind me and walked to the side of the room. Sinking onto the bed, I opened the top drawer and rummaged through her belongings. Once I finished going through the last drawer in both the nightstands, I made my way into her closet. I found no hidden items or journals. Then it dawned on me. When I was a teenager, I kept a diary hidden under my mattress.

I slipped a hand under the mattress but didn't find anything. Moving around to the other side of the bed, but there was nothing there either.

My body sank onto the bed, feeling defeated. Staring down at the floor, my eyes spotted something unusual. I stood and walked over to the wall looking down at the floor below the Drake poster hanging on the wall. Kneeling, I touched the wood panel along the wall. The piece of wood wasn't sitting snug like it should be.

I pushed down on it.

The wood was loose.

Ten

Using my fingernail, I pried the board up and set it aside. I leaned forward and peered into the hole then reached a hand inside, feeling a little scared something would attack me. There was something hard and thick at the bottom, like a book. I wrapped my fingers around the object and pulled it out. Sitting back on my heels, I held what I believed to be her diary. My eyes traced over the cover as I ran my fingers over the stressed brown leather binding. There were no words written on the cover indicating that it was a journal.

Shame and fear washed over me. I swallowed, my mind spiraling on what to do now that I had found her book of secrets. These were her private thoughts that no one was supposed to see or know but her. Was it wrong of me to go through her things? She wasn't here, not that it made what I was doing okay. It was still wrong in every sense, but I was her mother and I needed to know why she did what she did. Any mother would do what I'm about to do, wouldn't they? They would want to know the truth so they could fix things. To make sure it would never ever happen again.

Moving my index finger to the corner, I flipped the cover open. There were no words written until several pages into the book. It was dated May 2021. Three years ago. That would have made Mia fourteen years old.

Scanning down the page, I read every other word. There was nothing that caught my eye but your normal teen drama. Girls she liked and ones she didn't. She mentioned a boy named Jacob and her best friend Kat from next door. Apparently, Kat had caught Mia kissing him. Even though she mentioned that he had kissed her first. Kat didn't want to hear her excuse and now Kat wouldn't speak to her. I had never heard about this, but then again how would I? It wasn't something her and I would have talked about. We didn't communicate, period. Especially personal things like this.

Searching in the back of my mind, I couldn't recall Kat being at our house much after high school started. Had they had a fallout because of this? I read on.

Further down the page, Mia had written how upset she'd been about what had happened and that she tried to talk to Kat, but Kat wouldn't have anything to do with her. I turned the page, reading more of what had happened. There were a couple more pages about how Mia felt, but then it changed to when she met Trevor.

I leaned back, pulling my legs out from under me and pushed myself back against the bed frame. Although I still felt like I was betraying her trust; our relationship wasn't solid like a rock. We were far from being mother and daughter of the year. But from here on out, I was going to change that. I would make Mia talk to me. She had too.

The suicide attempt was our awakening. This was a way we could start a new relationship. A relationship we should have had many years ago. It wasn't *too* late, was it? I had had this talk with many of my patients. They would all be ashamed of how wimpy I was being. That I didn't do what I preached. In fact, I was doing the total opposite of what I told them to do.

Focusing back on the journal in hand, I turned the page. Mia had written about her first time with Trevor. A tear streaked down my face. I had always wanted to be a mother that had a relationship with her daughter. One that could never be broken. We would sit and talk about life and the things that bothered us. We would tell each other our secrets. But we weren't anything like I had always imagined we would be, but I could only blame myself.

I skimmed over the next few pages not wanting to meddle, but wasn't I too late? Hadn't I already invaded her privacy? She didn't have to know what I was doing. I wouldn't ever tell her I had read her diary. I would keep this to myself.

Snapping out of my thoughts, I looked back down at the book in hand. She wrote about our family trip to the Bahama's last month. About missing Trevor but she also wrote about how much she loved laying on the beach and listening to the waves.

A door slammed downstairs, and I dashed over to the hole and replaced the board. Scurrying to my feet, I hid the diary under my shirt. I hurried to the door listening before I opened it. Poking my head out, I didn't hear any sound of someone coming up the stairs. I slipped out of Mia's room and raced to my bedroom, closing the door behind me.

Eleven

The following morning on my way to work, I pulled into the parking lot of T.J. Maxx and drove to the back where the delivery trucks parked. The same parking lot I had been coming to every day this week.

Shifting into park, I turned off the engine. My hand slipped between the door and the gray leather seat. Pressing the control button, I laid flat, staring up at the dark gray cloth tightly lined along the roof of my car.

I closed my eyes. Not to sleep but to forget. Though I knew I would never forget what happened that day almost three weeks ago. How had I missed the signs? Sure, I could blame it on work and the fact that I was never home as often as I should have been. I wasn't just her mother but a psychiatrist too. I should have known, right? Yes, of course, I should have. Mothers and daughters have a bond and can sense when things are wrong. But that was the thing, we weren't like most mothers and daughters. Not like Mary and Katherine Palmer, Mia's best friend from across the street. Now they were the mother and daughter of the year. Well, *were* as in past tense. Mary had passed away in May a couple of months ago and I had lost my best friend.

Mia and I had a good relationship, at least I thought we did. Sure, I was stern with her. I had to be. It was the only way to make her strong like me. She was almost an adult and would be heading out into the world on her own. She needed to be ready.

Mia was rebellious. I, too, was once a teenager. I hadn't wanted to be around my parents either. Always locked away in my room or sneaking out after dark to be with friends and going to parties.

But still, I should've known, right?

Maybe I could have prevented it from happening. Wasn't that my job? I listened to people's problems every single day, and yet here I was sitting in my car wondering where I had gone wrong with Mia.

How had I missed the signs?

Would I see them if it happened again?

Will it happen again?

Would I be able to save her? The questions blogged my mind. How hadn't I known that something was terribly wrong.

When it came to my son Ethan, I had nothing to worry about. Well, not until recently with what I found in his room. He was always a go-getter. He didn't need my attention.

Did she do it for attention?

Was she trying to get me to notice her?

Of course, I thought about her every day. But maybe that was the problem. Maybe it was my fault because I didn't show her enough love. I knew this and yet, I couldn't accept the truth. I believed there was more I could've done.

The rewind button in my brain was stuck as I replayed the reason I had gone into Mia's room that night. It was like a force pulling me down the hall. She had asked me repeatedly not to barge into her room.

"Mom, can't you knock before you come in? What if I'm naked or something? God, Mom!" Mia had shouted at me more times than I could remember. She was so melodramatic when she hit her teens. So, I had knocked first, but she hadn't answered.

I almost turned and walked away not wanting to disturb her taking a bath or whatever she was doing in her room. But something drew me to that spot, wanting me to go inside. The cold metal knob against the palm of my skin as I turned and opened the bathroom door. My eyes were already looking down at the floor when I pushed the door open.

My chest tightened and I struggled to breathe. Then, as if I could fight them, the tears came gushing out. My weeping filled the interior of the car. I wasn't sure where it was coming from. Or how I still had so many tears left to cry. Does a person ever run out of tears? I was grieving, yet no one had died. Why was I so grief-stricken? I should be filled with joy, but I knew why my patients talked about these things in our sessions.

It was all my fault.

I needed to get it together. Mia will be home soon from the hospital. I reached over and rummaged through my purse until I found some Kleenex. I sighed, wiped away the tears and snot from my face. Pressing the button, I sat back up and looked into the rearview mirror. My eyes were red and swollen. I grabbed the cucumber cream I kept in my bag and patted some under each eye, soothing my puffy eyes.

Starting the car, I turned on the air conditioner, letting the cool air dry my eyes. I had ten minutes to get to the office before my first patient arrived.

Twelve

I sat in my office chair finishing the notes of my last two patients. I drew in a breath. My next patient would be here soon; that was if he didn't cancel. Though, if I were to be honest with myself, I crossed my fingers hoping he would. I didn't feel like being around anyone else today. Should I just go home? No, I didn't want to do that. Being in that house since it happened haunted me. And I was sure Scott wouldn't want to sell the place, at least not until Mia went off to college next year. Was she still planning on leaving?

As soon as the word college entered my mind so did the conversation from earlier that summer. The announcement that Mia and Trevor were moving to California. That they were both accepted into UCLA.

I didn't take the news too well. I stayed quiet, moving the food around on my plate trying to avoid the conversation Scott was having with them. How could he be so excited about Mia leaving us? I wanted nothing more than to storm out of the room to end the discussion, never to talk about it again. The truth was, it hadn't come back up since. Since the suicide, I haven't thought of anything else.

California. Mia never talked about wanting to go to college in a different state, especially thousands of miles away. What in God's name would make her want to leave and move so far away? The moment the words ran through my head, I knew why. Mia wanted to get the hell away from me. I should have realized that then, but I had become angry over the idea of my daughter moving across the United States. I hadn't even listened to why Mia had even wanted to go. Was I being selfish? Were there other reasons why she wanted to leave? Reasons that caused her to want to end her life?

Trevor, my mind fumed. I like the guy. He was a good kid, even after he lost his father years ago. But I wasn't too keen on him taking my little girl away from me. Even though my daughter and I didn't have the kind of relationship I had always wanted, but that was my fault. However, Mia played a part in it too. *It takes two to tango,* my mind quipped.

I let out a laugh. One that was unfamiliar to me. A laugh I haven't allowed myself to have in weeks. I knew being a teenager was hard; I got that. Been there done that as they say. The world sat heavy on my shoulders, and it weighed a few tons.

Then the suicide happened and... There was a knock on the door interrupting my thoughts. Olivia, the receptionist who had replaced Jackie, had been M.I.A. these past few weeks. She had done a great job but then had disappeared without even contacting me. Not one word. I had been taking care of all my calls and appointments.

Rolling my shoulders back, a ball of tension formed at the base of my neck. I wasn't surprised; I had been stressed for weeks. The knock came again. I stood, hurrying to the door.

~

An hour later, I shut the door and locked it. I was grateful to be done for the day. Three clients were my maximum on a Saturday, though Scott had told me numerous times to stop working the weekends and spend time with him. I really should. He wasn't the issue. It was me and everything I had witnessed. Everything I have found out since that dreadful day. Things I shouldn't keep to myself but can't seem to let them out. Things that Scott doesn't even know about. Things that could destroy what was left of our family.

Heading back to my desk by the window, I sat and opened the folder in front of me. *No interruptions this time*, I thought. I jotted down everything I could remember about the session I just had with my new patient.

Emotionally Withdrawn

Social Anxiety

Suicidal??

My hand froze in mid-air, staring down at the word. How common was this? Did everyone consider suicide? No, I knew that wasn't true. I had never thought about ending my life. Running away yes, but never suicide.

Even on the news there was always something about someone dying by self-harm, mostly teenagers. The statistics were high in Ohio. I had never considered my own child as being one of them. They were both so popular. Ethan with his football and Mia with her cheerleading and academics. I was sure there were no signs; but then again, I was never home, was I?

So, this was my fault—period! I have no one to blame but myself. I should have known she was depressed instead of shrugging it off as her being a teenager with raging hormones. Mia had a secret, and it was eating me up inside. The not knowing…

Setting the pen down on top of the yellow legal paper, I rested my head in my hands. I should have recognized the signs. Did that make me a bad mother? I had done everything in my power to *not* be like my father or my mother for that matter. Well, I certainly didn't treat my children the way my father had done to me. And I wasn't weak like my mother. But that wasn't what was troubling me. I didn't have to punish my children by locking them in a closet and not feeding them for days. I punished them by not showing them love and affection. That to me was the worst thing to do. Love was what formed a human into becoming a person. I wanted a friendship with my children, especially with Mia. To sit and talk about whatever. Going for mani-pedi's. A girl's day.

A tear slid down my cheek and dropped onto the notepad, smudging the ink. I didn't care. They were my notes; no one else would see them or read them.

My body folded into the chair. The wheels rolled backward, and the chair hit the framing around the window. My body jolted forward. I was tired. Tired of hiding and trying to be someone I wasn't. Did I still have time to change things? To be the mom Mia needed and wanted? A mother she deserved.

Yes, I could. There was still time.

She was still here and will be coming home tomorrow.

I had to fix things before it was too late.

Part Two

*I feel lost in this darkness that surrounds me.
Lost to the point of no return...*

Quote by Donna M. Zadunajsky

Mia
Now

Thirteen

My body sunk further into the mattress, feeling heavy and weighed down, but I couldn't recall how I had gotten into a bed. I strained to open my eyes, but they wouldn't budge. Last thing I remembered was climbing into my bathtub and... *Terror swam through my body.*

Was I dead?

Or had I survived?

How long ago was that?

What day was it?

A memory flashed in my head of my mom holding me. *How old was I?* Tears streamed down her face. *Why was she crying and yelling for help? What had happened?*

My ears perked up to the different voices surrounding me, but I couldn't understand what they were talking about.

"Sedation?

Suicide?

Three-week stay.

No family visits."

"Why would she do this Scott?" my mom asked.

"I don't know but they will find out. The doctors will help her, and she'll be back home in no time. I promise."

"How can you make that promise?"

My mom's voice sounded on the verge of tears. What was making her feel this way? Did something happen? Who are they talking about? Who needs help?

"Judith that's not what I…"

"I'm afraid you'll have to say goodbye now," a different female voice said.

"Oh," my mom muttered.

More sadness filled her voice. My heart fluttered with a yearning I hadn't felt in a long time. I wanted to reach out to her and hold her hand. Let her know that whatever had happened everything will be okay.

Silence filled the room. My head was fuzzy as I slipped in and out of consciousness. I had no idea what was going on.

I focused on opening my eyes; still heavy like I hadn't slept in days, weeks maybe. Through the slits of my eyelids there appeared to be no one in the room with me, but something else was different.

Forcing my eyes open, I scanned the room. The walls were a pale green instead of light pink like I had painted them when I was ten. A flat TV hung from the wall with a large bay window to my left. There was no mistake. I wasn't in my bedroom, but in the hospital.

I lifted my right arm to rub my eye. There was a bandage wrapped around my wrist. I turned and looked at my left arm and everything came flooding back to me.

I had gone through with it.

Fourteen

"Oh, good you're up," said a voice from across the room.

I turned toward the doorway. A woman I had never seen before with fiery red hair placed sloppily in a bun on her head and long slender legs walked toward me. She reminded me of the school nurse I had in Jr. High, except the school nurse was shorter.

"And you're sitting up. You must be feeling better?"

"Actually, I'm a little drowsy."

"Yes, probably from the meds the doctor prescribed to you." Her lips narrowed, "My name is Jeanette, and I will be your nurse today. Once you're able to, we need to get you up and moving. Can't stay in bed forever."

Inhaling a deep breath, I let my chest expand then deflate before carefully tossing the rough, scratchy sheet and white blanket to the side. I tried not to bend my wrists, in fear of ripping the stitches out, although the amount of bandage wrapped around my wrist was keeping it stable. Swinging my legs over the side of the bed, I scooched to the edge, letting my feet hit the floor.

"I don't think it's a good idea for you to get up if you're feeling drowsy," Jeanette stated.

"But you said I needed to get out of bed?"

"I said once you're not feeling dizzy."

I nodded, though inside I wanted to scream. "Well, I need to use the restroom anyway."

"Sure, I'll help you. Let's put these socks on your feet. They'll help so you don't slip on the floor when we're walking."

I stood after she slipped on the nonslip socks. The weight of my body pressing down through my legs to my feet, felt foreign. It had been a couple of days since I had been on them, at least I think so. I honestly don't know how long I'd been in the hospital. *Had it been days or weeks?*

I took a small step at first, just to make sure I wouldn't fall. "Umm," I hesitated, trying to form sentences from the scattered words in my head. "When did I arrive at the hospital?"

"Yesterday."

Yesterday? "When can I go home?"

"Well, I think you should talk to the doctor when he comes in to see you, but…"

"What?" I asked.

"The doctor told your parents that you will have to be admitted into the program for three weeks."

My head whipped toward her, and I stared blankly at the nurse. *A program? Three weeks?* "My parents left me here for three weeks?!"

"The doctor ordered you to stay. Your parents didn't have a choice. You do know you tried to attempt suicide, right?" Jeanette said, her words slicing through my heart. "When someone does what you did the state makes it mandatory for inpatient care, especially if you're a minor. Once you're able to move around without help, which should be in a day or two, you will then be able to attend group therapy."

I turned away from her. The state had put me in a Psych Ward for what I did. The truth was, I hadn't expected to live. I hadn't expected anyone to find me until it was too late. That had been the whole plan after all, hadn't it? Now I'm here and must face my family after what I did.

An image flashed in my mind. Her voice was soft and raspy as she spoke. It sounded a lot like my mom?

"Don't you dare die, Mia. I love you. You are my baby girl."

Why was she crying? I wasn't sure when this image in my head happened. Had my mom been there?

Had she found me?

Should I ask Jeanette?

Would she know?

I had so many questions but no answers.

My legs wobbled and my knees began to buckle. I teetered sideways and Jeanette tightened her grip, lifting me back onto my feet.

"Take your time."

Once inside the restroom, a light flashed on, making me squint. Blinking, I scanned the small room. A three-by-three shower stood in the corner with a floral shower curtain hanging half open. Soap residue streaked the white fiberglass walls, but otherwise appeared clean. The toilet sat beside the shower and in front of me was the sink. I shouldn't be surprised that everything in the room smelled of disinfectant, making the inside of my nose itch.

I glanced over my shoulder. "If you don't mind, I'd like to go by myself."

Jeanette looked at me quizzically. "Well, I'm not sure that's a good idea."

"I promise I will be careful."

"All right, I'll just be outside the door if you need me. But make sure you use the handrail and holler if you're having trouble. There's also a cord next to the toilet you can pull if you need help."

"Okay, thank you."

Jeanette closed the door, leaving me and my thoughts sealed away. I couldn't get the image out of my head. The cries from my mother echoing all around me. Her screaming for help. Then it hit me. My mom was the one who had found me.

"Oh, my God," I whispered, swallowing the acidic bile rising in my throat.

I had one hand pressed against the wall and the other gripping the sink as I took hesitant steps toward the toilet. Dizziness swept through me, so I sat down on the toilet and placed my head in my hands. My mind was filled with thoughts of my mom. *Had she* been the one who found me in the tub? Was she furious with me?* The words bounced around in my head.

"Please help!"

Those didn't sound like words from someone who was mad at someone, more like she was frantic, scared, terrified. My heart warmed, though I hadn't set out to get attention from my mom or anyone else for that matter. I hadn't meant for her to find me. I hadn't really thought about who would. I just wanted to end my life and forget about what *he* did to me.

"Mia, are you doing okay?" Jeanette called out from the other side of the door.

I jumped. "Yeah," I choked back the tears wanting to escape. I couldn't let Jeanette see me like this. I didn't want her to call the doctor because I was having a mental breakdown in the small, stinky, disinfectant restroom.

I flushed and stood in front of the sink. My pale appearance glared back at me. I slid my tongue across my lips, licking away the white, chalky coating that had formed on my teeth. Even my mouth tasted disgusting. I closed my mouth, making a *cluck* sound as my tongue smacked the roof of my mouth.

Grabbing the small plastic cup from the wall dispenser, filling it with warm water, I swished it around in my mouth before spitting it out in the sink. I did this several times along with rubbing my forefinger along my teeth to get rid of the plague build-up. After a few times of doing this, I then drank some water, filling it a couple of times. I couldn't believe how good the water tasted as it slid down my parched throat filling my empty stomach. I was unaware of how hungry I was.

The door opened behind me, and Jeanette's silhouette appeared in the mirror.

"You okay?"

I nodded because answering her would send me into a downward spiral. I shut off the water and tossed the plastic cup into the garbage can next to the sink before turning toward her.

Once back in bed I fell asleep only to wake hours later to voices arguing in the hall.

"You can't keep me here against my will," a voice screamed.

"Settle down, Jessica. No one is making you stay. You checked yourself in here, and you're free to leave when you want, but I don't recommend it. You need the program to help you."

"You don't know me! You don't know what I need! You don't know anything about me bitch!"

"Hey, there's no need for name calling. Let's go somewhere and talk. We don't want to upset any of the other patients here."

"Don't touch me! I can walk by myself."

The voices disappeared and the hall fell silent. I assumed they had left because I didn't hear them fighting any longer. There were no sounds of shoes smacking the floor outside my door.

I tossed the blanket aside and shifted my legs over the edge of the bed. My bladder was full and ready to burst. I cautiously took small tentative steps toward the restroom and closed the door behind me.

As I sat on the toilet relieving myself, I thought about what my family must think about me. And Trevor? Did he know? He was probably going out of his mind wondering why I did what I did. I hoped he didn't blame himself. He didn't do anything wrong.

I held onto the wall, making my way back to the bed when I heard a familiar voice out in the hall. My head whipped around. I stared at the door, waiting for it to burst open.

"Sir, you can't be here."

"I need to see her."

"I'm afraid that's not possible."

"Tell me what room she's in!"

"Security, can you get him out of here, please" the female voice said.

Gripping the bed rails, I sat down on the edge of the bed. *He didn't know what room I was in, did he?* No, I clearly heard him ask what room number. I held my breath waiting for the door to swing open and see him standing there, but the door didn't open.

My body wilted as I exhaled, sinking further into the mattress. My body wilted as I exhaled, sinking further into the mattress. His words repeated in my head from that night, *Tell No One.*

This hospital was the only place that would keep me safe from him. I had to do whatever I could to stay in here to stay safe, because it was the only place I felt safe right now.

Fifteen

A few days ago, the hospital moved me to a new facility. Jeanette had said it was for my own safety but didn't tell me why? I hadn't tried to kill myself again so what did she mean by, *"for my own safety?"* Whose safety was she talking about? Me or someone else's? There was no way to ask her because she didn't work at this facility.

There also hadn't been any more attempts of *'him'* getting in to see me. Maybe that was what she meant. Had he tried again? I wasn't sure. It was probably better that I was here then. My new nurse Kathleen said I will be going home in a couple of weeks; something I was dreading. Although I missed Trevor so much! My dad was probably going crazy and surprisingly I did miss my mom too.

I'm just not sure I can handle being out there where he can hurt me again. Why hadn't I paid attention to his odd behavior before. The stalking and long stares. I hadn't told anyone and wasn't going to. They wouldn't believe me if I did tell them, would they? I mean, even as I think about it, I wouldn't believe it myself, but it happened, and it was real.

I sat cross-legged on the bed when a knock resonated through the room. My head jerked up toward the door. My body relaxed when the person entered the room. I needed to stop being so scared. This was the safest place for me.

~

"Hey, Aiden," I said.

Aiden and I had met in my first group therapy session when I arrived here. I was grateful we were only allowed to use our first names in this place. There was no one here from my school, but that didn't mean they wouldn't know me by my last name. I was popular at my high school, and I was a cheerleader. I've been to hundreds of football games. I was sure someone would know me here but none of the faces looked familiar to me, making me feel at ease. I didn't need the whole school knowing what I did because then they would start asking questions. Questions I didn't want to answer. But I also knew it would be inevitable since gossip spread fast in the town I lived in.

Aiden and I didn't talk at first. Like we were scoping out the group before we talked about why we were here in the first place, though I hadn't been truthful. I hadn't told anyone the real reason I tried to end my life. I'm not sure I'll ever will tell anyone.

"Mia, what are you doing?" Aiden asked.

"Just trying to come up with something to write in this journal they gave us." I held up the book, waving it in the air.

"Right? Do they really expect us to pour out our hearts in that thing? Like it will heal us?"

I laughed. "If only that would fix *us*."

Aiden walked toward me and climbed onto the bed, facing me. She had long, slender legs with a small blue jay tattooed on the inside of her right leg just above her ankle. She wore long sleeves, most likely to hide the cuts on her arms. I'd seen her pulling the fabric down to hide the scars, but not before I had seen what looked like a different tattoo on her left wrist. Or maybe it was a birthmark. I hadn't had time to get a good look at it.

I looked down at my wrists, now free of the bandages, but they still had the stitches in them. I'm looking forward to having them removed in a few days. The doctor said that they were healing very well.

"You feel like taking a walk outside? We can check out the pond," she suggested.

"Sure, sounds nice," I shrugged my shoulders.

"Don't sound so enthused about it."

"Sorry, it's just…"

"Just what?"

"I haven't been outside since I was admitted into this place."

She nodded but looked at me curiously. "Is there a reason you're scared to go outside?"

I laughed, masking the fear that stirred inside me. My stomach clenched at the thought of *him* out there. Would he be waiting for me? How would he know when I'd go outside?

"Nope, no reason. Let me just get my shoes on." I quickly hopped off the bed, walking toward the closet. It was August outside, so I knew the temperature would still be warm and I wouldn't need a jacket.

"Yeah, okay. I'll meet you outside my room in a few minutes," Aiden replied. She flung her long legs over the edge of the bed and stepped off.

Her presence lingered behind me for a minute, until the sound of her sneakers left the room. She wasn't buying into my answer as to why I was hesitant to go outside. She had caught me off guard, and I didn't have a response ready. I was sure she wouldn't be the only person who would find it weird that I didn't want to go outside. I'd have to play it cool. The chances were slim he'd be outside waiting for me, but then again, I shouldn't take the chance. But…but if I'm not alone then he won't try anything, right? I hated feeling this way. I loved being outside. I missed being outside. And now he had ruined it for me. I will never feel safe again.

One of the male nurses followed us outside. Apparently, we weren't allowed to be outside without supervision, making me feel like I was in a prison or something. *A prison for the crazies,* I thought, almost laughing out loud. Did they think one of us would try and run or maybe they were afraid one of us would try and drown ourselves in the lake? Is that weird how I thought about that? Was that how my brain was programmed now? Looking for more ways to kill myself? In truth, I didn't really want to die. Then I'd never see Trevor again, even though I should break up with him. Besides, he wouldn't want me now. I'm damaged goods.

A warm breeze swept across the lawn, blowing the blonde strands of my hair into my face. My eyes closed, allowing myself to relax and soak in the warmness I hadn't experienced in a while. I pushed the hairs back behind my ears and opened my eyes. Water splashed beside me, and I turned to find Aiden standing at the edge of the lake skipping rocks. I walked over to her, bent over, and gathered a few pebbles in my hand.

"I haven't skipped rocks in forever," I said.

Aiden tossed another rock. "Every summer my dad and I would go out to my grandfather's lake house, and we'd sit on the shore, skipping rocks. We sat for hours at a time, neither of us saying a word."

"That sounds nice."

"It was."

"What about your mom?"

"She died when I was three. My dad raised me my whole life. I don't know what I'd do without him."

I nodded, feeling the same way about my dad too. We were a team, him and me, and something I wish my mom and I were.

Sixteen

"So, tell me, Mia, do you think you're making any progress since you've been here?" Dr. Hardy asked.

My lips formed into a smile, pushing my cheeks up. I wasn't sure if I could pull it off, but Aiden said I had to make them believe I was doing fine even if I wasn't. It was the only way I would get out of this place in two weeks, otherwise they might try and keep me here longer and that wasn't going to happen if I could help it. I needed to be with Trevor.

"Yes, I actually feel more like myself," I lied. In truth, I couldn't stand looking at myself in the mirror. The feel of *his* hands on me. His hot breath creeping along my skin. His words slithering their way into my ear as he threatened me.

Bitterness entered my throat as the images of that night came racing back to me not that they were ever gone. I would never forget that night. The memory would always be there haunting me. I never wanted to relive that nightmare ever again.

I swallowed, feeling the hot, sour liquid going back down my esophagus while still holding the pasted smile on my face, praying Dr. Hardy couldn't tell that I was faking the smile and was about to puke. I turned away from his cynical eyes and grabbed the glass of water on the table beside me, guzzling the entire glass.

"You feeling, okay? You look like you're about to be ill."

My eyes shifted to the floor. I couldn't look at his judging eyes, knowing he wouldn't understand. How could he? He was a man. A man with needs. A man that if provoked would do whatever he wanted to get his way. Though, I couldn't be sure Dr. Hardy was just like *him.* I didn't know him well enough. In fact, I knew nothing about the man sitting at the desk wearing an ironed, white, long sleeved dress shirt. His salt and pepper hair was combed in a sleek comb-over off to the right.

I set the empty glass down on the side table and swallowed the last of the water I had in my mouth. I closed my eyes waiting for the sick feeling to subside. This was something I used to do whenever I felt car sick. I squeezed my eyes tighter, wishing the thought away because it wasn't what I needed to be thinking about right now.

"No, I'm fine," I finally choked out. A heat wave washed through my body, drawing sweat to the surface along my hairline and my armpits.

"I know you want me to believe you are doing well, Mia, but you're not as good at playing these charades as you think you are. You know it's my job to be able to observe people. I've been doing it for over twenty years now," he said, tapping his pen on the wooden oak desk. "Anything you say in this room is confidential, Mia. No one will ever know but me. You can trust me."

Could I? As much as I wanted to tell someone what happened to me, I just didn't feel safe. *He* haunted my dreams at night, and I've lost a significant amount of weight before the suicide and more since being in here. My clothes were now two sizes too big for me, if not more.

"I'm just not ready yet, Dr. Hardy. But soon, I just need more time." He needed to believe me even though I was never planning on telling him what had happened.

He nodded. "Well, you will certainly get that here. I want to see you again for another session in two days." He scribbled something onto the notepad in front of him on the desk. "You're dismissed. See you on Wednesday at 10:00 a.m."

I jumped up from my seat on the sofa and toppled forward. Dizziness swam through my head. My eyes flashed to Dr. Hardy, but he hadn't seen me, his eyes still focused on the notepad. His hand moving swiftly across the paper. What was he writing down about me? I hoped it wasn't anything that would keep me in this place longer than I wanted to be.

Turning away, I walked to the door, opened it, and stepped out into the hallway. The door *clicked* shut behind me and I rested my back against the frame, letting my muscles relax. The sick feeling faded, but only for a few seconds as the smell of eggs and bacon drifted up my nose. I bolted for the restroom down the hall.

I wiped my face with the back of my hand before pushing the lever down, flushing the toilet. Shifting my eyes away as my morning breakfast swirled then disappeared, replacing the toilet with clear water.

Gripping the chrome metal bar attached to the wall, I hoisted myself onto wobbly legs. My knees ached as I climbed to my feet. I hadn't thought about placing a towel on the floor. Since I had lost so much weight, there was nothing cushioning my kneecaps.

Usually, I didn't get sick. Had I caught the flu from one of the other teens staying here? This week had been the second time I hadn't felt good. Last night after dinner, I had thrown up. Yes, it had to be the flu.

I splashed water onto my face then peered into the mirror. My skin appeared milky white. The same look I've seen before when I had gotten sick. My body shivered as a chill coursed up my legs and out through the hair follicles on my head, making my skin tingle.

I hated feeling this way and wished my mom were here to make me feel better. Something she had always done when I was little. When had she stopped babying me? Well, I wouldn't say she babied me. No, that was something she did more with my brother than me.

I left the restroom and walked back down the hall toward my room. Once inside, I went into the bathroom, my stomach still woozy. After a few minutes the dry heaves stopped, and I stood, moving toward the sink. Laughter ricocheted off the walls, making its way into my room. I splashed water on my face, then wiped it away with a hand towel. Standing in the open doorway of my room, I scanned the hallway. The laughter seemed to be coming from one of the rooms at the other end of the hall.

    Turning away, I walked back into my room, closing the door this time. Part of me wanted to go see what had been so funny, but the other half of me knew it would be a bad idea to mingle with the others on this floor since I didn't feel good. I spent the rest of the day in bed.

Seventeen

Kathleen had come into my room several times throughout the day and night to check on me. She brought me a can of Sprite and some saltine crackers.

"This combination has always helped me feel better, and I've even given it to my kids as well."

"Thank you," I murmured. "I'm sure I'll feel better soon. It's just a 24-hour bug or maybe even something I ate."

She nodded before turning away and leaving the room. She stopped in the doorway, turned. "I'll check on you later."

My head moved up and down against the scratchy fabric on the pillow. Kathleen left without another word and my eyes closed.

~

When I woke, the room was in complete darkness. What time was it? How long had I been asleep? The clock was ticking somewhere in the room, but I couldn't see it. I shoved the blanket off my legs and pushed myself up. Although my body felt drained, the queasiness had subsided. I no longer felt sick to my stomach, which was a plus.

I stood, the cold floor pricking my bare feet. I must have removed the socks I had on my feet during my sleep. I slowly shuffled to the bathroom; thankful my eyes were adjusted to the darkness. A burst of light appeared and my hand flew to my eyes, shielding them from the bright light. I had forgotten all about the bathroom light being on a sensor. I wished there was a way to turn it off.

After a minute of rapid blinking, I hurried to the toilet and sat down. Once I finished urinating, I wiped, flushed, and washed my hands in the sink. Walking toward the bed, I was thankful to have the light from the bathroom lighting my way. A creak came from somewhere in front of me. My eyes flicked toward the far corner of the room blanketed in shadow, then a silhouette of a person came into view.

My body stiffened.

My stomach dropped.

I stood frightened like a deer in headlights.

Was *he* here?

How did he get in here?

How long had he been in this room watching me?

I took a hesitant step backward, putting as much distance between him and me as I could. Then the room collapsed into darkness, and I stood immobilized with fear. The light in the bathroom had turned off. Maybe he hadn't seen me because he hadn't made a move toward me. I hadn't gotten close enough to see if he was asleep.

It wasn't him, my mind quipped. My throat tightened, making it hard to swallow. "Breathe," I whispered. If he was asleep that meant he didn't know I was awake. I needed to get the hell out of this room and find one of the night nurses. My head jerked up when I heard my name. My insides quivered.

"Mia is everything okay," Aiden's voice filled the room.

My body wilted like a flower deprived of water. "Where are you?"

The legs of the chair scraped against the floor. "Right in front of you."

Before I knew it, Aiden's arms wrapped around me, holding me tight. She helped me to the bed. The mattress sunk under our weight as we both sat down. The thought of him being here in this room vanished into thin air. I choked back a sob.

"Are you okay? Kathleen told me you didn't feel well."

"Yeah," I croaked, my throat completely dry. "I was just feeling a little under the weather."

"Well, I'm glad you're feeling better now. I was worried about you when you didn't come to group earlier today."

I had forgotten all about group therapy. "I'm sure no one else missed me," I laughed.

"You'd be surprised."

I didn't respond.

"When the nurses called lights out, I snuck out of my room and into yours. I've been sitting in the chair for hours. You were so out of it. I didn't have the heart to wake you." Aiden released her arm from around me.

"Oh, I hadn't heard you come in last night." My mind flashed back to all the times I hadn't known *he* was around. All the messages left behind for me to find. A chill ran down my spine when I thought of him being so close, when I hadn't felt him near me.

I turned toward Aiden who sat quiet and unmoving. "You never told me why you're here in this place?" I asked. Though to be honest, I hadn't told her my story either.

She turned to face me. "I was raped and then tried to end my life by taking a handful of my dad's sleeping pills. He found me hours later lying in my own puke."

My mouth dropped open. *She was raped.*

Eighteen

The following morning when I woke up, the room was quiet. Opening my eyes, I scanned the area but didn't see Aiden anywhere. She wasn't sitting in the chair by the window or using the bathroom. I guess sometime during the night she had gone back to her room.

Suddenly, I had the urge to pee and quickly jumped to my feet, speeding to the toilet. The pressure on my bladder diminished. After washing my hands, I stood looking at my reflection in the mirror. My cheeks had color in them today which meant the flu had passed.

I stepped back into the room and peered around. There wasn't anything for me to do in here but to read or watch TV. I didn't have any of the things I had at home. A heaviness filled my chest as sadness washed over me. I'd been here for a week and already missed my house, my bed. But mostly, I missed Trevor.

My thoughts went to Trevor as I slipped back under the blankets. I missed the feel of his strong arms around me. The way he made my insides melt whenever he was around. The smell of his scent drove me crazy the second I inhaled it. But the same question I had been pushing to the back of my mind kept surfacing. If he knew why I had tried to end my life would he still want me? This I wasn't so sure about. He'd probably find me repulsive and break up with me the second he found out.

And what about my friends. Did they know what I had done? Were they gossiping about me? Did I really want to know? I didn't have my phone on me; something the hospital wouldn't allow me to have while being in this place. Which was a smart thing on their part, but I would like to know what was going on outside these walls. Not that I wanted to know the words they were probably calling me on social media. What they all had to say about me. If they were even talking about me at all, but I've lived here my whole life; I knew whatever happened in our town spread like wildfire. There was no doubt I was the talk of the town. I had no control of the thoughts in their heads, but I had an idea. I was one of those people who always had an opinion about what others did or didn't do. I didn't hesitate to start a rumor about someone. Oh, how the tables have turned and I'm the outcast now!

My thoughts drifted away from my fellow classmates. They weren't who I was most afraid of. I knew once I left this place, I wouldn't feel safe out there. Not if *he* was out there somewhere:

Watching.

Waiting.

Would I ever feel safe again? Or would I have to keep looking over my shoulder to see if he was there, waiting to harm me again? That didn't sound like a life I wanted to live, but then again, I did try to end my life to get away from him. Though, I don't think I'd try it again or maybe I should. It would be the only way to escape him.

Trevor slipped back into my mind. As much as I loved him, there was no way I could be with him. Even if he never knew the truth. How could he want someone like me who had been attacked and violated in such a horrific way? Touching me would disgust him. Would Trevor think I had provoked the person to do what he did? Part of me didn't think so, but I had never been in this type of circumstance before, so I wouldn't know.

A knock sounded on the door of my room, snapping me out of my thoughts.

"Mia, are you feeling better this morning? Will you be able to eat breakfast?" Kathleen asked, sticking her head inside the doorway.

"Yes, I feel a lot better," I replied from the comfort of my warm bed. "I'll be there in a minute."

She nodded and continued down the hallway.

I climbed off the bed and padded to the bathroom. After a quick shower, I slipped into a pair of black sweats my mom had brought from home. I pulled the t-shirt over my head, smelling the gain detergent she used to wash our clothes.

Once out in the hall, Aiden was standing with her back against the wall, no doubt waiting for me to come out of my room. To be honest, she seemed to always hang around my room. I was sure she just felt relaxed around me. Felt safe. We had gotten close this past week. She told me things I didn't feel comfortable talking about, but she didn't hold back anything.

"Hey, when did you leave my room last night?"

"Just after you fell asleep, then I went back to my room," Aiden said, pushing herself off the wall and walking toward me.

I nodded. "Did you get any sleep?"

"Some."

I waited for her to continue, but she said nothing more.

We walked down the hall toward the cafeteria. It wasn't huge like the lunchroom at school, mostly because there weren't hundreds of people here. I think it would be weird if there were. That would mean there were more kids like me and Aiden. Not that there weren't. Some don't come here or go through with the whole suicide thing. Some actually succeed.

~

The trays were stacked upside down near the far wall. There were several different choices of food, so you weren't stuck eating the same thing all the time. I preferred cereal over eggs anyway, but even cereal was getting old.

I grabbed a glass of orange juice and set it on my tray. Sliding the brown plastic tray along the rollers, I reached out and snatched a plate of pancakes under the warmer. They wouldn't be as good as my dad's, but I needed to try something different.

"Let's sit by the window today," Aiden said.

I nodded and followed behind her. After setting my tray down on the small, multi-colored, laminated, square table, I pulled the chair out and sat down. Looking out the window, the sun cast rays of light between the tree branches. It looked amazing from this view. I wished I were outside soaking in the last of the warm weather. Though it was the first week of August, we technically only had a month left before fall arrived.

Picking up the glass of orange juice, I took a few sips, then placed it back down on the tray. My eyes scanned the table but saw no maple syrup.

"I'll be right back. I need to find the syrup for my pancakes."

Aiden didn't respond. Maybe she hadn't heard me. It didn't matter anyway. Less than a minute later, I was pouring syrup over the stack of pancakes on my plate. I'm not going to lie. They weren't half bad, but still not as good as my dad's either.

Sliding my tray through the opening in the wall near the garbage cans, I stepped aside waiting for Aiden to follow. She seemed to be moving in slow motion and hadn't talked at all during breakfast. Had I said something to her that offended her? I shook the thought away. No, I hadn't said much to her since she was in my room last night. Or maybe, it had nothing to do with me at all. Clearly, she was in here for the same reason as I was. Depression and suicide. So maybe, maybe she was going through something she didn't feel comfortable talking to me about. Although she did tell me she was raped. In all reality, I wasn't being all that forthcoming with her.

Aiden's thin, tall figure towered over me as she came and stood beside me. We both turned and fell into step alongside one another, neither one of us speaking still.

"Hey, umm, did I say something wrong?" I asked.

"No."

"Oh, okay." Pain clamped a tight band around my chest. There was no eye contact, which meant she was lying to me.

Nineteen

The muscles constricted in my throat, trapping the scream inside. My cry for help lodged in my throat as a hand pressed hard against my mouth. I fought to get away, but *his* strength overpowered mine. Kicking my legs, but I wasn't making any contact with his body to get him off me.

My body leapt upright, making the springs in the bed *creak*. My eyes sprung open, searching the room but finding nothing. He wasn't here. It was just a dream. A really, really bad dream. A nightmare my subconscious mind kept replaying over and over. My breathing slowed, feeling relieved that I was still in the hospital. *He can't get you in here,* I reminded myself, though not believing the words.

I sank back against the pillow, my insides sagging with relief, yet exhausted at the same time. I wasn't sure how long I could live like this. The nightmares were becoming a nightly thing, and I didn't know how to stop them. Well, I had tried but failed, that was how I ended up in here.

Throwing back the covers, I slipped out of bed and padded to the bathroom. It felt like déjà vu from the night before, but Aiden wasn't in here like last night. She must have fallen asleep, something she has been needing these past few days or maybe even longer. She had dark circles under her eyes and her fragile figure showed that she hadn't been sleeping well at all. When it was time to eat, she always picked at the food she placed on her tray, only nibbling on a few bites here and there. Come to think of it, we were just the same. We both had dark circles under our eyes and had lost weight. Was she having nightmares too?

I dried my hands and headed back to bed. There was nothing else to do, and I wasn't sure what time it was. The room was too dark to see the clock on the wall although I could hear the ticking of the hands. I crawled beneath the blankets and stared up at the ceiling, until I eventually fell back to sleep.

∼

Days slipped away, which meant I was closer to leaving this place behind. The bed was far from the mattress I had at home. The springs were poking my bones leaving my body sore. I had ten days left before I could leave and go home. Something I was looking forward to, but also something I was dreading.

A knock sounded on my door and Kathleen poked her head in.

"Good morning, Mia. How are you doing today?"

"Good actually."

"That's good. Are you coming to breakfast this morning?"

"Yeah, going to take a quick shower first."

"All right, see in the cafeteria," Kathleen replied, closing the door behind her.

The squeak of her sneakers told me she had left and was walking down the hall. I tossed the blanket to the side and made my way toward the bathroom.

~

Thirty minutes later, I was dressed and walking out of my room, stopping in front of Aiden's door. It was closed, so I knocked. There was no answer, so I knocked again, louder this time. Still no answer. Maybe she had gone to the cafeteria without me this morning.

I appeared in the doorway of the breakroom and scanned the room. I didn't see Aiden anywhere. The smell of eggs and bacon made my stomach growl, and I decided I'd eat first then go find her.

When I finished eating, I walked back down the hall toward the bedrooms. I knocked again on the door to Aiden's room, but still didn't hear anyone inside. Maybe she was sleeping and didn't hear me. I placed my hand on the knob and turned, pushing the door quietly open. There was a shimmer of light coming in from the window through the blinds. I stepped inside, looking at the bed, but she wasn't there. Flipping on the light switch, I stepped forward until I stood outside the bathroom, looking down. My high-pitched scream echoed through the room. I dropped to the floor next to Aiden. There was blood everywhere.

Footfalls pounded on the linoleum, stopping outside the bedroom.

"What is the matter in here?"

I turned and looked over my shoulder to find Kathleen standing behind me, her mouth gaped open.

Twenty

"Do you want to talk about what happened?" Dr. Hardy asked from his chair by the window.

The springs squeaked as he shifted his weight, sitting back in the chair. His glasses perched snug on the high arch of his nose. With his left arm outstretched and palm resting on the desk, he twirled the pencil between his fingers with his right hand before tapping the desk with the eraser end of the pencil.

The noise penetrated through the room to my ears. I wanted to shout at him to stop, but I wasn't sure I'd be able to stop myself once I started. The rage building up inside me was bubbling at the surface to get out. It was only a matter of time before I exploded but I liked Dr. Hardy, he didn't deserve that side of me, no one did but the person who had made me this way. He only wanted to help, but I don't believe I can be helped. I'm damaged goods. I'm not sure anyone would want me now or ever.

"Mia," he cleared his throat. He sat upright in his chair, elbows now on the desk, hands pressed together as if he were praying.

I could use all the prayers in the world.

"You shouldn't keep things locked inside. You need to let them out. You need to talk about what happened with Aiden."

It had been a week, and I hadn't wanted to talk about what had happened to my friend. It took a lot of coaxing from Kathleen, but I eventually climbed out of bed to attend these stupid sessions with Dr. Hardy. I shifted my body on the sofa, pulling my legs up and onto the cushion tucking them under my butt.

"You know I don't like shoes on my furniture, Mia."

Jerking my feet from under me, I pressed them firming on the floor. More irritated now than when I had come into this room. If he knew what was good for him, he'd shut his mouth before I shut it for him!

Fire ran through my blood like alcohol, which is something I wished I had right now to calm my nerves. I glanced up at the wall. The clock read 10:45 a.m. There was no way I would make it until 11:30 a.m.

"Do you not want to talk about what happened?"

I shook my head. Even though I did want to talk about it, I wasn't sure I could hold it together after I spoke the words. I didn't want to cry in front of him. I had never cried in front of him because I usually don't speak much in our sessions. Not about things like this, but nothing like this had ever happened before. I had never seen so much blood. All I wanted was to get the hell out of this place before I do what Aiden did—again.

To be honest, I thought she was fine. She hadn't showed signs of harming herself when she was in my room. Wouldn't I have seen the signs? I'm just like her. I had been through the same ordeal. Maybe after talking about what had happened to her, it brought up emotional things she couldn't deal with. She had to stop the thoughts from entering her mind by doing the only thing she knew how to do.

The only thing she could do.

The only thing I knew to do but failed.

"It's not your fault, Mia," he said, sitting up straighter, resting his arms on the desk.

"I never said it was!" I barked, then recoiled back into the sofa, wishing to disappear.

"Then why are you getting upset?"

"Because my friend tried to kill herself!"

Dr. Hardy's eyes flashed to mine then away.

My body stiffened. There was something in his eyes he didn't want me to see.

Had something else happened?

Did…did she die this time?

No! She couldn't leave me.

We were one and the same.

We needed each other.

It was the only way to make it through this.

Dr. Hardy sat back. "Do you think she tried to kill herself?"

Why was he asking me a question like that? Now I was the one staring at him. What was he saying? What was he asking? Did I imagine what I had seen in her room?

Slipping back inside my head, I scanned through the memories of that morning. I was sure I hadn't made it up. No, because it was real. I know it was. I couldn't have fabricated what I'd seen.

"Didn't she?"

The room fell silent, except for the *tick, tick* of the clock. I never noticed how loud the clock was before. My eyes shifted from the clock to Dr. Hardy, but he was looking down at the papers on his desk. Had he not heard me? I didn't want to repeat myself.

"You didn't know, did you?"

"Know what?" My brain ran through every conversation Dr. Hardy and I had, then it dawned on me. Was he talking about Aiden? "Know what, Dr, Hardy?"

"You'll need to talk to Aiden."

~

When my session was over with Dr. Hardy, I hurried down the hall toward Aiden's room. The door was open, so I stepped inside only to find the room empty. Not completely empty, the bed and dresser were still in the room, but all of Aiden's things were gone.

"Mia," a voice said from behind me.

I whipped around to find Kathleen standing in the doorway.

"Where's Aiden?"

Kathleen stepped forward until we stood face to face. "She's no longer here."

"What do you mean, no longer here?" My voice quivered. *She did it. She actually killed herself.*

"Oh, it's not what you're thinking. The doctors just thought it was best if she went to another facility," Kathleen replied, rubbing her hand up and down my arm.

Did she really think that was going to soothe me? "Why did she want to kill herself?"

"What?"

My eyes squinted at her. "I was talking with Dr. Hardy, and he said I needed to talk to Aiden about what happened in here, but you said she's gone. That..."

"I just told you she went to a new facility. Aiden's alive. She didn't try to kill herself, Mia. She..."

My body relaxed. Relief swam through me. "She what?" The words came out louder than I intended.

"I really shouldn't be telling you this but you both have gotten so close since you've been here. This is conf..."

"Just tell me!" I said through gritted teeth.

"Mia, Aiden didn't commit suicide, nor was she attempting too. She..." Kathleen swallowed. "She killed the baby she was carrying."

Baby? "She was pregnant?" My mind raced through each moment Aiden, and I were together. Had she mentioned the pregnancy? No, but she did say she was raped.

I gasped.

Twenty-One

I spent the rest of the day in bed not wanting to get out from under the blankets. Not wanting to exist in this place any longer. I had less than two days left before I could go home. A place I wasn't sure I wanted to be at either. Especially where it all happened.

Kathleen stopped by my room several times, but I told her I wasn't feeling well and thought it was best to stay here. She nodded and slipped out of the room, closing the door behind her. I wished she would stop checking on me like I would…

I wouldn't, you know. Try killing myself again. I understood why she wanted to keep an eye on me. I had to reassure her that I was fine. That I wanted out of this place, never to return. Besides, school was about to start in a couple weeks, and I needed to be ready for what my classmates were going to say to me or about me.

I also had to come up with a believable excuse to tell Trevor why we were over. I don't think he would believe I don't love him anymore. That would be a total lie, and I don't think I could say it to his face. So, then what should I tell him? He won't understand the truth. Maybe I could have my dad just tell him that it was over. Then I wouldn't have to face him.

I leapt to my feet and raced to the toilet, emptying the contents from my stomach. Oh God, was I sick again? Had I caught the flu from someone again? I hadn't eaten much in the past two days, so I wasn't sure what was wrong with me. Though it could be the thoughts of breaking up with Trevor. That or going home.

I stood, wiped my face, and rinsed my mouth. My complexion was pale, probably from the lack of sunlight these past few weeks. Another reason why I needed to get out of this place. The walls were starting to close in around me. I had to keep it together. Just a couple more days and I would be free from the wandering eyes that roamed the halls. Watching me like a hawk since Aiden did what she did. I still can't believe she was pregnant and… I don't know if I could ever do that to myself, but then again, I had sliced my own wrists.

The best thing for me was to keep myself busy. Keep my mind off what had happened. Which seemed easier said than done. But when I walked out of the bathroom, I went straight to the bed. Crawled back under the blankets and stayed there for the rest of the day and night.

Part Three

*A love between a mother and daughter
can never truly be broken...*

Quote by Donna M. Zadunajsky

Mia and Judith Two Months Earlier

Twenty-Two

Mia

My feet teetered back and forth as I swung on the swing my parents had hung on the porch when I was five years old. Hard to believe the years had gone by so quickly.

I picked at the paint flakes that had begun to peel on the arm rest, rubbing them between my fingers. The brittle chips crumbled and fell onto the wooden deck at my feet. When was the last time my dad had painted the swing? I couldn't recall but it had to be a few years now. The faded reddish-brown color had now turned to a dull rose.

A slight breeze blew the flyaway hairs from my ponytail into my face. Summer hadn't arrived, but the temperature was warmer than usual for this time of year. Not hot and sticky where your clothes clung to you, but according to the weatherman it would reach the upper 90's by the end of next week.

Today was starting to be a great day but would be even better once my boyfriend Trevor arrived. He had been working long hours this past spring and we hadn't spent as much time together as I would have liked. I knew he was saving money for our move to California next year. Which was one of the reasons why he was coming over today. We were finally going to break the news to my parents that we were moving there. Something I've been dreading. I was sure they weren't going to take it well.

Trevor and I had talked and talked about the different colleges we would apply to, and we chose UCLA. To be honest with you, I was nervous about going there for a while. Trevor had received a scholarship weeks ago. Even though we had applied to other colleges, his heart was set on going to California, and I wanted to make that dream come true for him. I wanted to go wherever he went, especially after he was offered a full ride, though we planned on getting our own place together after the first year of college. He was going to play football, hoping to get into the NFL one day. I was going to study nursing but hadn't made up my mind; becoming a physical therapist was also an option.

The tips of my toes brushed against the boards as I swung back and forth, making the chain *clank* against the hook. Chatter filled my ears. I turned toward the road; my neighbor Kat and her dad were coming out of their house carrying a large suitcase. There was only one suitcase, which meant only one of them was going somewhere. I hoped everything was okay.

Sadness squeezed my heart. Two weeks ago, Kat's mom had passed away from cancer. Even though we stopped being friends three years ago, I went to the funeral. How could I not go? Her mom was the best mom in the world, and it sucked that she died so young.

My mom and I aren't exactly mother and daughter of the year, but I still couldn't imagine her not being here with us no matter how much she got on my nerves. Who would be there for Kat when her wedding day came or when she got pregnant with her first child? A tear ran down my face and I wiped it away with the back of my hand. I wasn't sure why I was getting so emotional.

The car doors slammed shut and they drove away, leaving me here with nothing but my thoughts. My mind slipped away, thinking of my senior year and how epic it was going to be. There will be senior parties to attend and football games and cheerleading practice. This would be it, the end of high school and the start of Trevor and our lives together. But the best part, I would be away from my mother. All I had to do now was get through tonight.

~

"So, Trevor, how's your mom doing?" my mom asked.
"She's good."
"Maybe next time she can join us for dinner."
"Yeah," Trevor smiled. "Maybe."

I placed my hand on his thigh. Not only to let him know that I was here for him but to also stop his leg from jittering up and down. He didn't have to answer any of their questions, especially about his mom. Ever since his dad was killed two years ago outside Hank's Bar, his mom hasn't stopped drinking. Something she did to numb the pain. I didn't get it because drinking may numb the pain but the problems were still there. Besides, it wasn't known to everyone in this town that she was a drunk. She didn't leave the house except to get alcohol which she'd buy outside of town where no one knew her.

Taking a bite of food, I lifted my eyes and scanned the table. My brother Ethan sat quietly, picking at the food on his plate. For some reason he seemed distracted tonight. Not his usual joking self. Did he not want to be here? He was leaving in a few weeks for college, taking some early classes over the summer.

I looked over at my dad who took a sip of wine and placed the glass back down on the table. My eyes shifted back to Trevor who seemed to be somewhere else. I squeezed his leg, my signal that it was time to tell them the news.

He turned and looked at me. His eyes sparkled in the glow of the light hanging above the table. I closed my eyes and took in a deep breath, savoring the moment. There was no turning back once we told them the news. My mind had gone through every scenario of how this was going to go down. And to be honest, it wasn't going to go as planned if I knew my mom as well as I thought I did. She tended to overreact a bit. I wanted to laugh at that. She overreacted all the time, especially in the past year. I wasn't sure if it was work or a midlife crisis. Was she old enough to be going through menopause? And why was I thinking about this when I had great news to share?

Forks *clinked* against the ceramic white plates as I built up the strength to tell them. I swallowed the food I had just eaten, washing it down with some water. It was now or never. I looked back over at Trevor, he nodded.

"Mom, Dad, I have... I mean *we* have something to tell you," I said, glancing back over at Trevor, a smile spreading across my face.

The room fell silent.

My gaze swept across the table again, studying their faces. They stared over at us, their forks frozen in midair. To be honest I wondered what they were all thinking, but my answer came soon enough.

"Please tell me you're not pregnant?" my mom asked.

"Mom!" I shouted. "God, no I'm not having a baby." I watched her body sink into the chair with relief.

"Why would that be the first thing that comes out of your mouth? Besides, I'm not talking about my sex life with any of you."

"Thank God," Ethan muttered from across the table. "Spare us the gruesome details," he chuckled before taking a bite of food.

My dad cleared his throat. "Okay, so then what is it you two need to tell us. Is there a wedding we need to plan?" my dad snickered, winking at me.

Ever since Trevor and I started dating, my dad has always made the comment that we would marry someday, but we were too young for that now. Trevor and I had already discussed marriage and decided to wait until after we graduated from college.

Trevor shook his head. "No, actually I've been accepted into UCLA for next fall. I got a football scholarship."

My eyes darted around the table again, searching their faces. My dad smiled. My mom seemed to wear the same expression all the time before exploding. You would think being a psychiatrist she would think before opening her mouth and ruining everything, but then again maybe she only did that when it came to me. As for my brother Ethan, he was beaming with joy—shocking.

"That's so great, bro," Ethan roared.

My brother also played football, but I was surprised he was excited for Trevor since he didn't get a full ride to Ohio State. I'm not saying Trevor was better than him, but he did get us our first state championship trophy last year.

"Yeah, that's amazing. We're so proud of you," my dad said.

"I got accepted into UCLA too," I blurted out.

Silence filled the air, making my stomach twist into a knot. *Way to kill the mood.*

"Oh, I hadn't known you wanted to go to California. I thought you were going to attend Ohio State like your brother?" my mom questioned. Her eyes moved from me to Ethan, waiting for a response.

I looked over at Ethan, his face now red. Was he upset that I wasn't going to go to Ohio State? It was never carved into stone that I would go to the same college as him. Besides, we were kids when we talked about that. Things changed. I've changed. He had to know I would follow Trevor wherever he went, right?

"Well, I think that's great news, Mia," my dad said with a smile. He lifted his glass. "Let's toast to Mia and Trevor and their acceptance into UCLA. We are so proud of the two of you, and I know you will do great things with your life."

Beaming, Trevor, and I lifted our glasses and gazed at one another. The night turned out better than I had anticipated.

A chair scraped across the floor. My mom stood, threw down her napkin and stomped out of the room. Her footsteps echoed, smacking the wooden steps as she climbed the stairs. Seconds later, the bedroom door slammed shut.

Then again, there it was, my mom making everything about her.

Twenty-Three
Judith

Through my lashes, I see Mia pushing the food around on her plate. If I knew my daughter as well as I thought I did, it meant she was about to drop a huge bomb on all of us. Would it be a terrible thing to admit that my first thoughts were that she was about to tell us she was pregnant? I know they must be having sex. They've been together for years. It wasn't uncommon for teens to have sex, but I hoped Mia was smart enough to know better and took all the precautions necessary not to get pregnant.

A baby?

My head spun in different directions thinking and hoping it was something other than a baby. I prayed she wasn't about to tell us she was having a baby.

She was only seventeen years old. Too young to have a baby when she was still a baby herself. But maybe it was something else. I could only hope that it was. Had she decided not to go to college. Though, in this house, that wasn't a choice. My kids were going to be educated. Don't I have a right to protest that she goes to college no matter what she wants?

"Mom. Dad. I have…"

Mia's words sliced through the thoughts occupying my mind. I lifted my head, looking in her direction. She turned and glanced over at Trevor, a smile spreading across her face. She always had such a beautiful smile. One that would brighten up a room. Just that look alone was enough to tell me that I was right. I mean look at her glowing skin. Women who become pregnant always have such radiant skin. She was going to tell us, and our world would begin to shatter. And to make it worse, it was her senior year. She would be one of those teenagers walking down the aisle on her graduation day barefoot and pregnant, as the saying goes. All the other parents would look at me, whispering that I should have made them wait. They would think I'm a bad parent for allowing my daughter to have sex before she was eighteen. Not that I could've stopped her. Mia was a determined young lady. She had straight A's in school and was captain of the cheerleading squad. *Remember your teen years?* my mind quipped, but I shook the thought away.

My lips parted and my mouth opened. The words spewed out before I could stop myself. "Please tell me you're not pregnant?"

"Mom!" Mia shouted at me. Her face turning a shade of red.

My skin prickled from her outburst which wasn't anything new. I should be used to her behavior toward me. My body relaxed against the chair, relieved that she had said no about being pregnant. I was certainly not ready to be a grandma at the age of fifty.

Buried in my thoughts again, my head jerked up when the word wedding was said. A tightness squeezed my heart beneath the silk blouse I was wearing. Scott had always joked about the two of them getting hitched after high school though I hoped they would wait like we did and do it after college.

"No, Dad," Mia said, with a light giggle.

"I've been accepted into UCLA for next fall. I got a football scholarship," Trevor said.

I smiled; a flood of warmth ran through my body excited for him. Then it hit me, how will they make it work if Trevor lived in California? The miles alone would tear them apart. Mia wouldn't be able to live without him here.

"I got accepted into UCLA too," Mia blurted out.

The words stung as I absorbed them. Of course, she would go with him. Why would I think she wouldn't?

"Oh, I hadn't known you wanted to go to California. I thought you were going to attend Ohio State like your brother?" I questioned. My eyes moving from her to Ethan.

Ethan's face turned beat red. Was he angry that she wasn't following him? I had always thought they would go to the same college. They had always been close growing up, but I also knew things changed. Life did that. You could have everything planned out to a perfect 'T' but one little pebble in the road could take everything you had your heart set on and shake it up, sending it off course.

"Well, I think that's great news, Mia," Scott added. He lifted his glass. "Let's toast to Mia and Trevor and their acceptance into UCLA. We are so proud of the two of you, and I know you will do great things with your lives."

He always did that! Scott was different that way. He accepted anything that came his way, but not me. Change was not my strong suit. Before I could stop my irritation, I thrust the chair away from the table and threw my napkin down. The legs scraped across the floor as I stood, before plowing out of the room. I climbed the stairs. My footsteps smacked the wooden steps, before slamming the bedroom door shut behind me.

Twenty-Four

Judith

My eyes were on the book in my hand when Scott appeared inside the doorway. I was sure he and Mia had talked already. They always seemed to gang up on me whenever Mia wanted something. I couldn't tell if he was irritated at me for storming out of the room. I hadn't even finished my dinner. My behavior was unacceptable, but I couldn't sit there for another second listening to their childish scheme to move across the country. For what? Some college? Some scholarship? Trevor could've gotten one here and they could have stayed in Ohio.

The more I thought about the conversation, the more upset I got. Usually I could block out people, though in my profession, I try not to. Besides, they were acting crazy. California, really?

From the corner of my eye, I watched Scott walk toward the bed. My back was against the decorative pillows Scott, and I had seen in a display window in one of the small towns we had visited in Maine when we were in college. Just the two of us, embracing adulthood. He had spotted them first. The dark blue accent design matched the duvet comforter we had on our king-sized bed, so we bought them. *"Like my mother always said; if you see it, get it. You may never find anything like it again."* For me it was harder, I had to really want that particular item before I bought it.

He took a seat at the foot of the bed, taking my bare feet and placing them on his lap, rubbing my achy feet.

He looked up, his lips spreading into a smile. He was the handsomest man I had ever seen. My heart warmed, soaking in his scent, his touch. I don't know what I'd ever do without him. He was my anchor, keeping me grounded when I needed it, like now.

I knew what he was going to talk to me about. Scott and Mia were close, and I found him always siding with her when it came to certain things, probably more times than I could count. Part of me wondered if she did it to spite me because of how close Ethan and I were. Though Ethan was pulling away from me, possibly because he was an adult and in college. Not wanting his mom to baby him any longer. He was just so easy to please, unlike Mia who had Scott wrapped around her little finger since the day she was born.

"Hon, don't you think you're being a little hard on her?" Scott asked.

I started to shake my head but stopped. *Was I being hard on Mia? I had always wanted the best for her, but I knew how hard life could be for a woman, especially someone as young as my Mia.* "I wasn't trying to be Scott," I protested. "It's just that she always talked about going wherever her brother went. You know she followed him around everywhere when she was younger."

"Yeah, but she's heading toward her own path now, Jud. We as parents should accept that and allow her to grow. What would it accomplish if we stood in her way?"

He had a point. When I was her age, I wanted nothing more than to start my life. Mia was seventeen and would be eighteen soon. Adulthood was approaching sooner than I wanted. If I pushed her too far, then she would just pretend I didn't exist anymore. I couldn't live with myself if I treated her the same way my own parents did me, controlling everything I did. I basically ran like hell from them once I turned eighteen and graduated high school. All for good reasons, I might add.

My eyes were fixated on my hands lying on my lap. I felt like a little kid sometimes. Why was I pouting? I needed to stop this kind of behavior and act my age. I wasn't dumb. Scott would head straight to her room after we talked, making me the bad parent.

"It's only four years, then she'll be back here. I'm sure of it."

"What makes you so sure? She'll be with Trevor. Wherever he goes she will follow."

"Maybe so, but we must let her live her life. We can't always protect her."

"Why not?"

Scott chuckled. "Let me ask you about when you graduated high school. Did you stay or leave?"

He already knew what I did. I got the hell out of my parents' house and ran as far away as I possibly could and didn't look back. "You know she's going no matter what, so why are you in here?"

"Because, my love, I wanted to make sure you were okay. You are my wife, and you were upset about the conversation."

My heart sped with his words. "Thank you, but you didn't need to."

"I'm well aware of what I need and don't need to do. So, are you going to stand behind our daughter and allow her to live her life?"

I tried to stop my head from bobbing up and down but failed miserably. Did I really have a choice whether Mia could go or not? "I will love her no matter what she decides."

He stood and stepped toward me, bending closer, he kissed me on the lips. "Thank you. I'll go let her know."

The tap of his knuckles sounded on her bedroom door the minute he left the room. Once again, I was the bad parent because I didn't see things his way. He was so much more lenient, especially when it came to Mia. I'm not going to lie; I was jealous of what they had. Though, I guess I'm the same way when it came to Ethan. Was it wrong to have favorites? I know most parents will say they don't, but they do, one child always had one of their parents wrapped around their finger. Unless of course, you're a single child or you had parents who didn't give a shit about you and only cared about themselves as I did when I was young.

I opened the book in my lap. I wasn't really in the mood to read but I had to keep my mind from reeling. I wondered what they were talking about. Was he trying to get her to see things my way? Something Mia wouldn't do. I think sometimes she deliberately set out to hurt me.

The words blurred on the page before coming into focus. I reread the same sentence several times, my head not into the story. Was it wrong of me to want to know what they were talking about? Should I go listen outside her door?

No! Absolutely not, my mind quipped.

That would be childish. I wasn't about to sneak down the hall and eavesdrop. Scooting down, I leaned my head back against the pillow and closed my eyes.

I woke several hours later; Scott was lying beside me. I listened to his soft and steady breathing; thankful he wasn't one of those husbands that snored loudly all night long. In fact, I had never heard him snore once. I do recall times when I thought he wasn't breathing and would place my hand near his mouth or on his stomach. I tried to get him to do a sleep apnea test, but you know men, they think they're invincible.

Pushing the blanket to the side, only to realize that I wasn't under the covers. Scott had placed the blanket at the end of the bed on top of me. I sat up and placed my bare feet on the floor, listening to the sounds around me. The house was quiet.

Shoving my feet into my slippers, I padded to the bathroom and closed the door. A motion sensor lit the lights from under the cabinets as I walked toward the toilet. The lights were something we had installed years ago after seeing them at the store.

I flushed and stood in front of the sink. There were dark circles under my eyes from not sleeping well these past few nights. Usually, this was due to work. I wasn't sure why my brain didn't shut off when it was time for bed.

After drying my hands, I undressed, slipping into my nightgown. I turned the knob and stepped back into the bedroom. My left ear perked at a sound coming from out in the hall. Now standing at the bedroom door, I listened and waited.

There it was again.

A muffled sound.

Turning the knob, I opened the door and peered into the darkness, waiting for my eyes to adjust. Both bedroom doors were closed, but I could see a light coming from under Ethan's door. What was he doing up at this hour, although I had no idea what time it was? I hadn't thought about looking at the clock beside the bed, but it had to be late.

Stepping forward, the wood floor *creaked* and I stopped, waiting and listening. Had he heard me?

The door to his room opened and he stood in the doorway, his eyes darted in my direction. My mouth opened to say something, but then closed. There was something about his demeanor that frightened me. I took a step back and quickly closed the door to my room.

Twenty-Five

Mia

I had only been in my room for a short time since cleaning up the kitchen after dinner. I was thankful that Trevor helped me. Ethan left without even bringing his plate to the sink, not that I cared. He was acting weird tonight anyway. No wonder he and my mom got along so great. They were too much alike.

Sitting in my room, my mind replayed the events of the evening. Dinner had been quiet after Trevor and I told my family of our college plans. I shouldn't have been surprised that my mom stormed out of the room like she did. She seemed to always steal the spotlight, making everything about her. Didn't she care what mattered to me? That I wanted to be happy and doing so meant that I would follow Trevor to California? She would've done the same thing too if it were my dad. Wouldn't she?

I shouldn't care but I do. I've spent all my life starving for her attention, but Ethan always got that. Nothing I did compared to what he did or didn't do. He was the apple of her eye. To her, he never did anything wrong. He was the golden child.

"Whatever," I muttered. He wasn't as innocent as she played him to be. There was a knock on my door, making me jump a little; my thoughts now disrupted.

"Yes," I called out.

The door creaked open, and my dad popped his head inside. "Hey, kiddo. Mind if I come in?"

"Um, sure." I pushed the book I was about to read aside. Here came the talk, which meant my mom must have made him come into my room to change my mind about moving across the country to go to school.

He stepped inside and closed the door, something he never did. He stood gazing around my room as if he had never been inside before. He blinked, then stepped forward before sitting on the edge of my bed.

"Is everything okay?" I asked, forcing a smile as my stomach twisted into a tight knot.

"What?"

He was being weird. My dad never acted this way. He was usually very forthcoming, but something was up. "Dad?" I touched a hand on his arm.

"Sorry."

What was he being sorry for? Was he here to talk me out of going? I had no idea. "Dad, what's up? Why are you acting this way? Did something happen?"

"I talked to your mom about going off to California," he said, turning to look at me.

"I'm going and there's nothing she can do about it! Besides, what does she care anyway? She doesn't love me," I snapped, my blood boiling inside. *What the hell! Why can't I do what I want?*

"Mia! Your mom does love you." There was emotion in his blue eyes.

"Well, she never shows it. Ethan is her favorite."

"That's not true and you know it."

"Whatever. I'll figure out a way to pay for it myself if I must. I'll take loans out and pay them back." *I don't need her or her approval.*

"Mia, we have college money set aside for you."

"Yeah, but I don't get the money if I go to a school that I want to go too? If I go to UCLA? That's bullshit!"

"Hey." He gave me a stern look. "Don't use that tone with me young lady. She's your mom no matter what and I don't like you talking this way about her. You both need to solve this issue between the two of you. Get whatever is bothering the two of you out in the open. She loves you, just the same as your brother."

Please, I thought. I looked at him and then down at the bed. His words were slicing through me. He was defending her over me. But he was right. We did need to fix us, but I wasn't making the first move. She was the one that needed to apologize to me.

"No matter which college you choose to attend, you have the money we put aside for you. We just want what's best for you. If your heart is set on going to that school, then I guess we will have to accept your decision. We just thought you would stay here. Stay in Ohio."

"It's not like I'm running off with some stranger. It's Trevor. We've been together for years."

"Yeah, but you've always talked about going to Ohio State."

"Things change. I changed. Besides, they have a great nursing course out there."

"Nursing?"

"Yeah, they have a separate building built just like a hospital where you work on medical simulation mannequins that are programmed like humans. This way you can learn from your mistakes if you accidently do the wrong thing. Alarms will sound."

"Wow! That does sound amazing. I didn't know you were looking into being a nurse."

"I guess I'm just full of surprises," I smirked. "Dad, what's the big deal with me leaving?"

"Nothing, I actually came into your room to tell you she's good with you going to California, but you wouldn't let me talk. If it's what you really want, then we will stand behind your decision."

I reached over and hugged him. "It is what I want."

"Then I guess it's settled," he smiled.

"She'll think I put you up to letting me go."

"No, she won't. Just promise me you'll come home to visit."

"Dad? Yes, of course I will."

He reached over and gave me a kiss on the cheek. "I know you'll do great things, Mia. You're so smart and have a good head on your shoulders."

"I wish Mom saw what you see."

"She does. She just doesn't show her emotions when it comes to you kids. She's getting better though."

I wondered who he thought he was talking to. Because she sure wasn't any different with me. She didn't say the words "I love you".

"Don't stay up too late."

I gave my dad a look.

"I know, I know. You're not a kid anymore, but you'll always be my baby girl," he said with a wink. He opened the door and slipped out, closing it behind him.

The mattress squeaked as I bounced with excitement. I was going to California!

Twenty-Six
Judith

On Monday morning, the house was surprisingly quiet. Scott had left for work an hour ago and the kids must still be sleeping.

I stood in the kitchen drinking a second much-needed cup of coffee. Staring out the kitchen window, my mind shifted back to last night when I came out into the hall. I couldn't shake the feeling I had about Ethan. He didn't say a word to me, but the look on his face was terrifying enough that it made me shiver. I couldn't recall a time when he looked at anyone, especially me, in that way before. His icy, cold stare was with eyes that could burn a hole through your soul.

It hadn't occurred to me until this second that he could've been angry, but at me? I hadn't done anything wrong; well, not that I could recall. It couldn't be because I walked away from dinner last night, which had nothing to do with him, but Mia and the conversation. Nor could it be that I had woken up and come out into the hall last night. I had the right to be anywhere I wanted in the house. So, after Ethan had caught me out in the hall and the death stare he had given me, I hurried back inside my bedroom, pressing my back firmly against the door. I waited until the faint sound of his door clicked shut before exhaling the breath in my lungs.

Part of me wondered if I should mention it to Scott, but then decided not to. I was sure it was nothing. He was a teenage boy. Although nineteen, he still had raging hormones in his body that switched on and off like a light switch. Were all teenage boys like that? A memory flicked in my mind when Scott and I were in college. He was, as I recalled, a bit of a horny dog back then. I let out a small giggle at the memory. After having Ethan and Mia, sex wasn't as often as it used to be, especially with our busy schedules.

As I sipped my second cup of coffee, I replayed the conversation Scott and I had had before leaving our bedroom this morning.

"We should take a family trip somewhere this summer," I stated.

"That sounds nice. Where do you have in mind?"

"I was thinking maybe the Bahamas. A long-needed vacation for the family before Mia leaves for California."

Scott smiled. "That does sound relaxing." He brushed my hair to the side and kissed my neck. "We could use some alone time," he whispered.

Oh, how I missed the touch of his breath against my skin which aroused my inner core. I closed my eyes, letting the sensation flow through me. It had been a while since the last time we had sex. Work had been busy for both of us; that and the kids.

"Yes, we can."

Rinsing out my coffee cup, I placed it inside the dishwasher and headed toward the garage door, grabbing my bag as I went. I slipped into the leather seat and started the car. Pressing the button on the visor, the garage door ascended. Once I backed out of the driveway, I headed in the direction of work, which was no more than twenty minutes away.

In my rearview mirror, I saw Ethan's car parked at the curb, which meant he was still home and probably still sleeping since he was up so late last night. Well, I wasn't about to spend the rest of my morning dwelling over last night's event and turned on the radio. Pressing the music app on the touchscreen, the sound of a saxophone flowed through the car speakers and into my ears. My body relaxed into the plush seats as the music filled the car.

Before I knew it, I turned into the parking lot and parked under the light pole near the side of the building. Most days, it was dark when I left work. I was usually the last to leave. I never liked to leave my work unfinished for the next day. Notes had to be typed into my patients' files of what we had discussed in the appointment. I also tried not to take any of my work home with me. Something Scott and I had agreed on after we were married.

I glanced around the lot, noticing only a few cars this morning, not recalling my schedule for the day. My kids and their lives had fogged my head, and I was unable to think for once. I had to let last night go and focus on what I needed to do today.

Twenty-Seven
Mia

Vacation?

My dad told me the following afternoon we were all going on a vacation to the Bahamas. It did sound nice, but I didn't care for them not letting Trevor come with us. According to my dad, my mom said that it was a family vacation. Did that mean she didn't consider Trevor family? Or was she doing this to get back at me for the whole college thing? I figured she would find some way to punish me for choosing to go off to California. What a bitch!

"It'll be nice," my dad said as we sat in the kitchen, just the two of us. "The warm sun on your skin and the sand between your toes. Can you picture it, Mia?"

"What are you, reciting a country song right now?" It did sound nice, but I still wished Trevor could come with us. He said he was fine with it and had to work anyway. I won't have anyone to spend my time with except Ethan and the way he's been acting lately, he wasn't going to be much fun.

"Zac Brown Band," my dad laughed, nudging my arm. "It's just a week Mia, then you'll be back here and can spend all the time you want with your bae."

Did he seriously just use the word *bae* to refer to my boyfriend? "Dad!" I retorted.

"Well, isn't that what your kids say nowadays?"

He had a point, but still, parents aren't supposed to use words like that, especially when talking to their kids. "Yes, but just don't, Dad. It's not parent-like to talk like that."

"Parent-like?" he questioned, scratching the side of his head.

I snorted a laugh. "Yeah." My dad was a cool guy. Always trying to be like us. Like a teenager. I bet he was fun when he was my age.

The front door opened and slammed shut with a *thud*, making the walls rattle. Ethan was home. Lately he seemed moodier than usual and spent more time in his room, doing God knows what. I didn't know what was troubling him, but I hoped he didn't bring it on our trip. Was that why he was mad?

We both turned and looked at one another waiting for the wrath to come from Ethan. His heavy footsteps smacked the wooden floor. He didn't even stop as he passed the kitchen doorway. Our heads turned in his direction, listening as he stomped up the stairs, then the slam of his bedroom door echoed throughout the house.

"Well, your brother is home," my dad mumbled.

"Yep, I hear that."

"Maybe I should go talk to him. See what's up."

I shrugged my shoulders. "It's your funeral."

My dad cackled as he scooted off the chair and stood.

"Rest in peace, Dad," I laughed. "Rest on peace."

He shook his head and marched out of the room and up the stairs. He knocked on Ethan's door. My cell phone chimed. It was Trevor. I read the text message before climbing off the stool and heading outside. Trevor's car was sitting at the curb. I skipped down the steps and slipped into the passenger seat.

"Hey, you," Trevor said as I turned toward him, a smile on my face.

He reached over and kissed me on the lips, his hand smoothing my cheek before his fingers tucked my hair behind my ear.

I let out a sigh and smiled with my eyes closed. Everything I had been hoping and dreaming for, every fantasy of my long and dull life, was coming true. Well, maybe not dull life. Every day with Trevor was an adventure.

"So, what do you want to do today?" Trevor asked.

"I don't care as long as I'm with you."

"I have just the place."

Trevor pulled away from the curb and drove toward town. I squeezed his hand, then laced my fingers between his. He lifted our hands and kissed the back of mine. What will I do without him for a week? I didn't want to think about it. I still had two weeks before we were leaving and would spend every second I could with him.

The trees and houses whooshed by before Trevor pulled into the vacant school parking lot. The pavement was riddled with cracks as he drove to the far corner of the lot and parked. The football field was one of my favorite spots where we would go to be alone. We climbed out of the car. Trevor popped open the trunk and grabbed a blanket and a bag.

"What's in the bag?"

"You'll see," he smiled.

I had no doubt it was something romantic because that was how he rolled. I linked my arm with his and we strolled to our spot on the fifty-yard line.

"Fried chicken and watermelon," I squealed.

"But not just any fried chicken."

"Your mom's famous country fried chicken?"

He bobbed his head.

"Is she feeling better?"

"No, but today was one of her good days."

"You need to get her to see a psychiatrist or a therapist but not my mom of course, someone else. She needs to talk to someone. She can't keep drinking the way she is." What was I doing? Was I turning into my mom trying to give advice on how to help his mom? God, I hoped not, but I wasn't wrong. His mom did need help.

"She's depressed."

"I know, Trev, but it's been two years since your dad died. You have to talk to her. What happens after you leave next year? Did you think of that?" I didn't mean to come off sounding rude or demanding, but the words were out there now. I couldn't take them back.

"I know. I'll try and talk to her again."

I couldn't tell him that my worst fear was his mom killing herself after we left for California. I could never say that to Trev; he would never forgive me for thinking such a thing. Trevor and I had been together for a couple years now and we told each other everything. I nodded, not wanting to ruin our time together with unpleasant words. If Trevor said he will handle it, he will take care of it. I leaned in and kissed him. "Sorry babe," I whispered on his lips.

We sat for hours on the football field, talking about whatever, mostly California. The last of the sun dipped behind the rows of trees, light dancing between the branches. He wrapped his arms around me and held me close. The sun disappeared, leaving us in thickening shadows. The light at the edge of the field hummed then blinked on. My eyes skimmed the football field, stopping at the bleachers. I wasn't sure, but I swore there was someone there, hiding in the darkness, watching us. I couldn't see them, but the hair on my arms told me different. I rubbed my eyes and looked again. This time there was no one there. Just my imagination getting the best of me.

"Hey, you okay?" Trevor asked with concern in his voice.

"Yeah, just thought there was someone out there."

Trevor turned looking in the direction I was staring. "Where?"

"I thought I saw someone behind the bleachers, but I'm sure it's just the shadows of the trees."

"I don't see anyone."

"Me neither." Though I still couldn't shake the feeling I had. Who would be out here besides us? It wasn't just our place, it belonged to the school, so it could've been another student wandering around, but at night? Didn't matter. Whoever it had been was gone now. If there had been anyone there at all.

Twenty-Eight
Mia

The plane touched down, jolting me from my slumber. It had been a long flight, and I hadn't slept well the night before, dreading every second I would be away from Trevor. We haven't been away from one another more than a day at a time.

I reached over and lifted the hard plastic shade, letting sunlight filter in as the plane wheeled down the runway toward the terminal. The sky was a radiant shade of blue with no visible clouds in sight. Right now, all I wanted to do was lay in a chair on the beach, listening to the waves smack the shore. The sooner this vacation began, the sooner it would be over with, and I could get back home.

"Mia, isn't it beautiful?" my dad said from beside me.

I nodded. "It's breathtaking."

I looked past him and across the aisle where my mom and Ethan sat. My mom had booked us seats in first class which wasn't anything new. She always had to have the best. Ethan had argued that he didn't want to sit next to me on the flight and had switched with my dad. Was he still angry because I wasn't going to college at Ohio State? Not that I cared, really. He would have to get over it sooner or later. I wasn't going to let him ruin my time here and would avoid him the entire vacation, if possible.

The intercom chirped. "On behalf of Delta Airlines, the flight crew would like to welcome you to Lynden Pindling International Airport. We will be arriving at the gate momentarily. Please remain in your seats with your seatbelt securely fastened until the aircraft has come to a complete stop at the terminal gate," the captain announced.

A half hour later, we were gathering our luggage and making our way outside to grab a shuttle to the hotel. The air was hot and sticky against my skin, and I tasted salt in the air from the ocean. Sweat beaded along my brow and I wiped it away with the back of my hand. My throat parched and I wished I had some water to drink.

The shuttle bus arrived and a tan man with white hair greeted us before loading our suitcases onto the vehicle. I took a seat at the back of the bus and stared out the window, watching the traffic zip by as we drove away from the airport and onto the highway. Before I knew it, we were pulling into a long driveway. The sign read 'Welcome to Atlantis Resort'.

I peered out the window, a monstrous building loomed in the distance. I had googled the hotel to find out what it looked like, but the view in front of me looked nothing like what I had seen on my laptop. It was paradise.

Once inside, my eyes grew wide as I took in the view of the lobby. A large open room with four sculptured pillars stood in the center. The place was beyond beautiful. Nothing I had ever imagined I would see or visit in my lifetime. Actually, I hadn't thought I would ever leave the town of Crawford, but that was all about to change.

I walked toward the center of the room as my parents waited in line to check us in. Tilting my head back, I gazed up at the ceiling studying the extraordinary artwork painted on the walls. It was awe-inspiring. I wasn't sure how they had painted such beauty of the Roman Gods and sea creatures. It was the most extraordinary thing I had seen since the field trip to the Cleveland Museum.

My cell phone chimed. Without taking my eyes from the view, I reached my hand back and slipped the phone from the pocket of my jean shorts. I looked down to see a text from Trevor. I clicked on the message.

Trevor: "Hey, did you land yet?"

Me: "Yes, just got to the hotel. It's so beautiful. I'll take some pictures and send them to you."

Trevor: "Can't wait to see them."

Me: "Wish you were here with me. You'd love it!"

Trevor: "Then we'll have to go sometime. Just you and me."

Me: "I'd love that."

"Mia, come on," my dad shouted from across the lobby.

I twisted around, rolling my two suitcases behind me, and headed toward the elevators on the far side of the room.

Minutes later, we were inside our three-bedroom suite with a view of the ocean. I wheeled my suitcases into one of the bedrooms. It had a queen size bed, TV, lanai, and my own bathroom. I opened the slider and stepped outside. The water was so clear and blue you could see all the way to the bottom of the ocean from up here.

"Mia, mom and dad want to know if you're hungry?" Ethan asked from the doorway.

I stepped back inside and closed the door. "Yeah, I could eat."

Ethan stood looking at me but didn't say anything. Sometimes he made me feel uneasy the way he stared at me, but *I wasn't going to let him ruin my vacation,* I repeated in my head.

Twenty-Nine

Judith

The hostess led us outside and we took our seats on the veranda. Tilting my face toward the sky, I soaked in the warmth of the sun. I couldn't recall the last time we took a vacation together as a family.

Looking across the table, I watched Mia texting on her phone, probably with Trevor no doubt. Part of me wanted to tell her to put the phone away and spend some time with the family, but I also didn't want to start a fight with her on our first official day in paradise.

"Hey, you okay?" Scott asked, squeezing my hand that was resting on the table. "You seem far away."

The feel of his touch sent electric waves through my body. I turned, a smile spreading across my face. "Yes, I'm fine. It's just so beautiful here, I got lost for a minute, soaking in the scenery."

"Yes, it is." Scott looked around, taking in the view of the ocean to his left. "It certainly is spectacular." He turned his gaze to Mia and Ethan. "So, what do you guys want to do after we have lunch?"

"I want to go down to the pool," Mia replied.

"You want to do the slide with me?" Scott asked Mia.

Mia scanned the scenery, spotting the huge slide off to her right. Her eyes widened. "Oh, I hadn't realized how tall it was from the pictures I'd seen online."

"Scaredy cat," Ethan chimed in, laughing.

"No!" Mia shouted.

If I know my kids as well as I think I do, the dare was on, and Mia would go on the slide. Just as the thought entered my mind, Mia chimed back.

"You're on. But I want to wait a couple hours after we eat before going on it," she said.

"Deal," Ethan replied.

When they were younger, the two of them would constantly make dares with one another. I was so afraid I'd have to explain why they were always getting hurt when I had to take them to the emergency room. The scar on Mia's right hand when she fell behind our house and cut her hand open, getting two stitches. And Ethan when he was about eight, he fell from a tree after Mia dared him to climb to the top. Thankfully he only got a broken arm out of it. It could have been so much worse. I was just thankful they had grown out of all that once they entered Junior High and made friends.

"I'll come with you two if you don't mind. I'd like to try out the slide." The three of them all turned and stared at me. "What? You don't think I like fun too?" I laughed.

"Mom, I'm not sure if you know what fun is," Mia said.

"I'm hurt by that," I replied, touching a hand to my chest. Though I can agree with her on that. I have been too busy with work things. Scott had sort of taken over the role of being the fun dad.

"I'll have you know that your mother does know how to have fun. We did some crazy stuff back when we were younger."

I let out a chuckle, shaking my head. "We sure did. I'm surprised we hadn't gotten caught on a few of our adventures."

"What kind of things did the two of you do?" Ethan asked.

I scanned my children's faces from across the table. What would they think of their mother being a rival? Some of the things I did were dangerous and stupid but thank God I hadn't gotten caught. My father would have locked me away in the closet for the rest of his life. But I didn't want to think about him. Not now, not ever.

"Well, before I met your father, the friends I hung out with, we would steal stop signs and toilet paper our classmate's homes." I wasn't going to mention all the parties I went to and the drinking I did back then. Some secrets were meant to stay hidden away, especially from our children.

"Mom, are you being serious right now?" Mia asked.

I nodded. "Why so surprised? You think I was always boring or something?"

"Umm, yeah!" Ethan said.

"I just can't picture you doing something like that. You always seem to be so perfect," Mia said, before turning her eyes away from mine.

That was one of the nicest things she'd said to me in a long time. In fact, I wasn't so sure why she was being nice to me. It had to be this place.

Thirty

Mia

Lying on a beach chair, I looked out over the water, listening to the sound of the waves crashing onto the shore. The sound was therapeutic to my ears. I grabbed my phone and took a picture, sending it to Trevor with a message that said, "Wishing you were here with me." I waited for his reply, but none came. I placed my phone beside me and closed my eyes, soaking in the sun.

"Why are you sitting out here and not at the pool?" the male voice said.

I sat up and turned to see who was talking to me. It was my brother. I rolled my eyes which he couldn't see behind my big, dark sunglasses. Couldn't he go somewhere else? The beach was miles long and he had to come to the exact spot where I was?

"What do you want?" I asked, flopping back onto the lounge chair, looking out over the ocean.

"You know, Mia, you're turning into a real bitch lately."

I chuckled. "Whatever. Like you've been a pleasure to be around lately too."

Sand sprayed onto my bare legs, sticking to the suntan lotion I had put on minutes ago. I whipped my head toward Ethan. "What the hell!" I shouted.

Ethan kicked at the sand again I turned away, shielding my face.

"You're such an ass, Ethan!"

He stomped away, mumbling under his breath.

I grabbed a handful of sand, throwing it where he had stood. God, he was acting like a child. What was his deal lately? It couldn't be because I announced that I was moving to California, could it? Well, he'd have to get over it because I'm going whether he liked it or not. It was my life, and we weren't little kids anymore. I didn't have to follow him around and go wherever he went. I can make my own decisions and do what I want.

My phone chimed and I picked it up. There was a text from Trevor.

> **Trevor: "Hey, beautiful. The view looks amazing."**
>
> **Me: "God, I miss you. What are you doing?"**

I smiled. My mood instantly changing as my heart fluttered with warmth.

> **Trevor: "Miss you too. Just got home from mowing a few lawns. Taking a shower then heading to the hardware store to help Mr. Paxton."**
>
> **Me: "Busy man."**

Trevor: "Yeah, must keep busy while my girl is gone. Well, gotta go babe, love you."

Me: "Love you too."

I sighed, hating that our conversation was over at least for now. Just like that, he was gone again. I typed in a few kissing emojis then flipped my phone over and closed my eyes again.

This time next year, Trevor and I will be lying on the beach together in California. I smiled as I pictured us lying there soaking in the Cali sun. Just the two of us. No parents to tell us what to do. No annoying brother to scold me because I don't want to follow him to Ohio State. I shook my head. What an ass Ethan was being. And he was the mature one? I let out another laugh, shaking my head.

~

"Mia, come on. We're going to be late," my mom hollered from the doorway of our hotel room.

I flicked off the light in the bathroom and walked out of the bedroom. This morning, I was wearing a flowered wraparound skirt with a white tank top, which not only covered my bikini but also accented my tanned skin and flip flops.

"You look pretty, Mia," my mom said, holding the door open for me.

"Thanks," I replied, shuffling out into the hall. I hadn't seen my mom in such a good mood in a very long time. It suited her.

I hoped she stayed this way the rest of the trip. It was nice not fighting with her for a change.

Twenty minutes later, we all climbed out of the rental car at the marina. My dad had rented a boat for the day. I hadn't known he knew how to drive a boat. Though the question had never come up for me to ask. With both parents busy and Ethan and my extracurricular activities, there was never any time to go on a vacation.

After placing the coolers onto the boat, my dad started the engine and we pulled away from the dock and into the open waters. My skin soaked in the sun as I laid on the flat dock. I applied sunscreen with a bronzer, giving me a darker look. If I was going to be in the tropics, then I was returning home looking the part.

I laid back onto the bow and closed my eyes. A shadow appeared above me. Shielding my face with my hand, I squinted to see who it was. Ethan stood in front of me.

"What do you want, Ethan?"

He didn't say anything, he just stood there staring down at me.

"You're blocking the sun," I shouted. Why was he being such a nuisance?

"Ethan, leave your sister alone," my dad said from the back of the boat where he was steering.

Ethan turned away and headed to the right side of the boat and took a seat. I laid my arm back down at my side and closed my eyes, shaking my head at the same time. What the hell was that all about?

Hours later, we all sat around eating lunch. Except for the odd behavior earlier, Ethan hadn't said anything to me since yesterday, but that was fine with me because I really didn't want him to ruin the mood I was in. If he wanted to have a rotten attitude on our trip, then that was his problem not mine.

Later that night, I jerked awake to find someone standing at the foot of my bed, staring at me.

Thirty-One
Judith

"Mia, come on. We're going to be late," I said from the doorway, though the words came out louder than I intended. Knowing Mia, she'll think I'm mad but I'm not. So, I will have to make sure my next comment comes out more cheerful. The last thing I needed was a fight. I wanted this trip to bring us closer, not further apart.

"You look so pretty, Mia," I said, holding the door open for her as she walked toward me.

"Thanks," she replied, a smile spreading across her face.

When was the last time she smiled like that at me? Her beauty blossomed when she smiled. When she was younger, I told her all the time how beautiful she was, but school and work took all our time. It became harder to see her, especially in a good mood like she was now. The teenage years were stressful, not for only her, but me too. My daughter would be leaving the house soon, venturing off on her own and turning into an adult.

Mia strode out into the hall, and I pulled the door closed, twisting the handle to make sure it was locked. Placing the room key inside my bag, I padded down the hall behind her. Our flip flops were slapping the bottoms of our feet as we hurried toward the elevator. Scott and Ethan were already downstairs waiting on us with the rental car to take us to the marina. I can't recall the last time he took me out on a boat. He never ceases to amaze me. My lips spread into a smile. I shifted the cooler to my other hand which was packed with food and drinks.

Less than a half hour later, we all climbed out of the car and headed toward the boat dock. Once the coolers were placed onto the boat, Scott steered us out into the open water. The warm air caressed my skin and I was thankful I did a French braid this morning to keep the wind from tangling my hair.

Glancing around, I spotted Scott standing at the steering wheel with his sunglasses perched high on his nose. He looked so handsome standing there. Maybe tonight, him and I could have some alone time while the kids hung out at the pool or something. I was surprised at the thoughts in my head. It had to be this place. The warm weather and salt water around us; it was better than I had expected. I couldn't have imagined a more beautiful place for us as a family to spend a week.

Looking toward the front of the boat, Mia sat lathering her skin with lotion. Her skin was getting darker even though we have only been here two days. I won't tell her that she took after me. My friends in high school were always jealous of me whenever we went to the beach. It never took me long to get a tan.

Looking over my shoulder, Ethan sat along the side. He was looking at Mia, then his eyes dropped down at the floor of the boat. Was he still upset with her about college? After thinking about what Scott told me about Mia going to nursing school, I wasn't as upset as I was when she broke the news to us. I just wanted her to be happy and, of course, have a good education.

A nurse.

I couldn't stop the excitement bubbling inside me. Though I will miss her. She was probably glad to get away from me. That was why I decided on this trip. Besides, we haven't gone anywhere as a family in God knows how long.

~

We pulled up to the dock before sunset. Though it would have been amazing to see the sunset on the water, Scott had agreed to have the boat back by six that evening.

Once back at the hotel, we all slipped inside our rooms and showered before heading downstairs for dinner. Although I was exhausted by the day's events, dinner on the veranda sounded nice and we would still be able to watch the sunset after all.

"Do you know what you want to eat, Mia?" I asked as she browsed over the menu.

"I think maybe grilled fish and lobster."

"That does sound good," Scott replied.

"What about you Ethan? Do you know what you want?" I asked.

He dropped the menu onto the table. "I think the sauté grouper," Ethan replied.

"Another great choice," Scott said. "What about you, hon? Do you know what you want?"

"You." The word slipped out before I could stop it.

"Mom!" Mia shrieked. "So not appropriate. Did you forget that we are sitting here?"

The heat rose in my cheeks as I lifted my head and smiled. "What? Your father and I love each other. What's so wrong with that?"

"Nothing is wrong. It's just I never hear you talk like that around us," Mia replied.

My eyes shifted to Ethan who hadn't said much of anything this whole trip. I wondered what was going through his mind. Was he stressing about starting college? Now that I thought about it, I had noticed a change in him in the past couple months. He spent more time in his room or stayed out later than usual. I would have to make time for him and maybe get him to open up. That was if he would talk to me, which was something else that had changed. We used to talk all the time, but lately he had been closed off. I made a mental note to spend some alone time with him tomorrow.

Thirty-Two
Mia

A chill ran through me like an electric current, making the hairs on my arms stand straight up. Once my eyes adjusted to the darkness, I was able to see who the person was standing at the foot of my bed. What the fuck was my brother doing? Why was he standing there staring at me? Why was he even in my room, period!? Was he sleepwalking?

"Ethan," I choked out. My eyes searched his face. "What are you doing?"

He didn't move. He just stood there watching me, his eyes unblinking.

"Ethan," I said a little louder, hoping not to wake our parents.

Shoving the blankets to the side, I slipped out of bed, creeping toward him. I have read never to wake someone who was sleepwalking.

The moonlight glistened through the glass slider, lighting my way down the side of the bed toward him. I reached out with a shaky hand and touched his arm. I didn't have time to react when he turned toward me and gripped both my arms, pulling me into him. His lips pressed hard into mine. I tried to push him away but couldn't break free from his grasp. His fingers were digging deeper into my skin. I raised my foot and kicked him in the shin. His fingers loosened and I stumbled backward toward the bathroom door. If he moved one step closer, I would scream and lock myself inside the bathroom.

"Get out of my room!" I growled. He stood there for a few seconds before limping out of my bedroom. I hurried to the door and closed it behind him, locking it. With my back pressed against the door, I slid to the floor, tears cascading down my face. *What the hell just happened? Why would my brother do that to me? Obviously, he hadn't been sleepwalking. He kissed me. Surely, there was a good reason why he had done what he did, right?*

Using the back of my hand, I wiped away the tears and walked into the bathroom. I flicked the switch and closed the bathroom door, locking it. The bedroom door was locked but right now I needed to feel more secure.

~

The following morning, I found myself lying on the bathroom floor, shivering. I had no blanket, just the tank top and shorts I had worn to bed last night. I must have fallen asleep in here.

Pulling myself up, I stood and stared at my reflection in the mirror. My appearance was pasty. My eyes dropped and I noticed marks on my arms. These were finger marks from Ethan gripping my arm, and…and then I recalled him kissing me. I swallowed, feeling sick again.

The bruises were faint but would be darker as the day went by. How the hell was I going to hide this from my family? The weather here was extremely warm and wearing something other than a tank top or even a T-shirt would be too hot, but I had no other choice. Makeup wouldn't work because I would sweat it off. I couldn't tell my parents what had happened last night and was sure it would never happen again. But I was still going to find out why he did what he did. My brother had never in my entire life done anything sexual to me. Maybe he had been drunk. Didn't matter. He had no right to touch me like he did.

"Mia are you up?" my mom's voice came through the closed bedroom door. The door handle rattled in the background. "Why is this door locked? Mia is everything all right in there?"

Shit, I forgot about the bedroom door. I threw open the bathroom door and grabbed a sweater from the chair beside the TV stand and put it on.

"Mia?"

I unlocked the door and opened it. My mom stood tall. Her eyebrows drawn together.

"I'm fine, I was just getting changed."

Her eyes moved down my body. "But you're still wearing your pj's?"

I glanced down at my body. "I mean, I was about to get changed."

"Oh, okay. Well, we're getting ready to go downstairs for breakfast."

"I'm not hungry."

"Are you sick?" She raised a hand, placing it on my forehead. "You're not hot, but you do look a little pale considering how tan you've gotten since we've been here."

"Just go without me. I need to shower anyway. I can meet you guys downstairs later."

"Are you sure?"

"Yes."

"You don't think it was the food you ate last night, do you?"

I started to shake my head, but then shrugged my shoulders. "Yeah, it's possible," I lied. "Just text me when you're done eating."

"Well, okay if you're not hungry then we'll see you in an hour. Meet us in the lobby."

I nodded and pushed the door closed but not before I saw my brother standing in the living room. His eyes set on mine. My stomach dropped and I quickly closed the door, locking it again.

With my back against the door, I closed my eyes. I didn't want to be here any longer. I wanted to go home, but we still had four more days before we were leaving.

~

Thirty minutes later, I turned off the water in the shower. My body felt disgusting and unclean, and I wanted nothing more than to scrub away my brother's touch. My cell chimed and I walked over to the sink and picked up my phone. My stomach dropped. It was Trevor. I could never tell him about what had happened last night. How could I? The tart taste of acid crept up my throat, but I swallowed it down.

Tapping the screen, I read his message.

Trever: "Hey, beautiful. How's your morning going?"

A smile spread across my face at his words. God, I missed him so much.

Me: "It's good and yours?" I lied.

My stomach tightened. I hated lying to him, but I couldn't tell him what happened. Would he think I caused it? No, definitely not! Trevor wouldn't, would he? Doubts began to race through my head. Trevor and I could talk about anything, but this; this he can never know about.

Blood entered my mouth when I bit down on my bottom lip. The guilt building up inside me. No one can ever know about last night. I had to keep it a secret no matter what. Besides, they wouldn't believe me anyway. My mom for sure. It would just be another reason for her to hate me. For a split-second, I wished my mom would stay with me instead of going downstairs with them, but she had already left the room.

Thirty-Three
Judith

Mia's reaction surprised me. She had always been a breakfast person. I hoped she wasn't catching the flu or something, then the trip would be ruined, and she would spend the rest of the time in our hotel room. I wouldn't want to do anything either because I would want to make sure she was okay, not that she would want me hovering over her. Teenagers hated their parents hanging around them. Knowing Mia, she would stay in bed on her phone texting with Trevor.

Though, it could be that she misses Trevor. Come to think about it, they haven't spent more than a day apart from one another. Young love. God, do I remember those days. The quick eye glances at one another as you're walking by from across the room. The glowing warm fuzzy feelings that stirred inside your belly with anticipation of the next time you're together. I shook my head. Yes, it was probably just her missing Trevor and not the flu.

I stayed in the hotel room hoping I could change Mia's mind while the guys headed downstairs to get us a table in case it was busy this morning for breakfast. It was Friday and more vacationers were arriving every day.

I slipped into my room and used the bathroom. It was spacious, almost the size of our room at home. The walls had a floral wallpaper pasted along the ceiling. No doubt to give you that tropical feel.

Once I finished, I padded out of the room and stood outside Mia's bedroom door. The sound of water came through the walls. She was in the shower so that meant she would be downstairs when she was finished. The bright sun glimmered through the glass slider, pulling me toward the lanai. Once outside, I closed my eyes and listened to the waves rushing onto the shore before being sucked back out to sea. My muscles relaxed to the calming sound. Taking in a deep breath I exhaled, letting the feeling envelope me. It had been a long time since I had a relaxing day. No work to pass my time, but wasn't that what vacation was all about?

Minutes later, I stepped back inside and stood outside Mia's door again. Raising my hand to turn the knob, my hand stopped in mid-air. What was I doing? Mia would have my head if I barged right in without knocking first.

I leaned in, pressing my ear to the door, the sound of water was still running so I decided I'd go downstairs and meet the guys while Mia got ready. Besides, I didn't want to rush her if she was having a hard time, nor did I want to get on her bad side. The Mia yesterday on the boat was someone I hadn't seen in a very long time, and I liked it.

I pressed the button near the elevator. My mind still stuck on Mia, I couldn't shake the feeling that something wasn't right, but I couldn't put my finger on it. It'd been a long time since we used to talk about anything and everything. How could I get her to talk to me? How would I start a conversation?

Twisting my neck, I glanced over my shoulder, hoping to see Mia walking toward me, but there was no one in the hall. The elevator chimed and the doors opened. Stepping inside and placing my hand against the metal, I looked out once more before accepting that she wasn't coming down with me. Should I stay up here with her, maybe have a girl's day and the guys could do something else together?

Before I could stop myself, I stepped off the elevator and walked back toward our room. Hotel card in hand, I held it against the lock until there was a *click*. My hand pressed down on the handle, pushing open the door.

Mia's door was still closed. I stood on the other side anticipating what to do next. My hand hovered over the doorknob before dropping to my side. I didn't want to intrude and decided I would give her some space. Wasn't that what moms did? I turned and walked back out the door.

The elevator seemed to stop at every floor before finally arriving on the first floor where the restaurant was located. Making my way through the lobby, I spotted a line of vacationers standing impatiently in line waiting to check in. Scott and Ethan sat in the far corner. Scott waved to me, and I hurried toward him.

"No Mia?" Scott asked, frowning.

"No, she said she wasn't hungry, so she'll meet us down here in an hour."

"I hope everything's okay," Scott mumbled.

"She's fine," I replied. "I think she just misses Trevor."

He nodded as if he completely understood what she was going through. "Yeah, you're probably right." Scott lifted the glass of orange juice and took a sip before placing it back down on the table.

My eyes shifted to Ethan. His eyes looked away, focusing on the menu in front of him. Even my son was acting weird. What was going on with my children these days?

"So, what are we doing today?" I asked.

"Well, Ethan and I were talking, and I guess it all depends on Mia, but we were going to have a guy's day while you and Mia did girl things," Scott replied.

A smile crept on my face. "That sounds like a wonderful idea." *How did he know that I was thinking the same thing?*

"Yeah, dad says we're going to rent jet skis," Ethan said.

"That sounds fun," I replied. "Maybe I can talk Mia into going shopping in town with me."

"I think she'd love that," Scott replied.

I hoped so too. The one thing I didn't want was to push her further away. Soon she'll be twenty-three hundred miles away from me. I wouldn't be able to see her or spend any time with her. Yes, it was a good idea. I just hoped Mia felt the same way.

Thirty-Four

Mia

Once outside the bathroom, I heard what sounded like a door closing. Had they all just left and went downstairs, or had someone come back into the room? Ethan? God, I hoped not. I waited, listening by the door. There it was again, but this time I was sure it was the sound of someone leaving the hotel room.

I quickly dressed and pressed my ear against the door, listening for movement. Nothing, so I turned the knob and slowly opened the door. My eyes scanned the room but saw no one. The muscles in my back and shoulders relaxed as I released the breath I had been holding.

More people clambered onto the elevator as I stood near the back awaiting my arrival on the main floor. The same place I knew *he* would be. My brother, I was sure, was sitting with our parents acting as if nothing had ever happened last night. I wondered if he was using his charm on our mom, making her think he was such a great son. Laughing and joking like they were the only ones in the room.

The image swirled in my head of him standing in my room last night and him…I couldn't even say it. It was ludicrous to try and comprehend what he was thinking at that very moment. I couldn't wrap my head around his motives. Did he have a motive? My stomach soured. Inhaling a deep breath, I held it before slowly letting it out, praying I wouldn't vomit all over these people in the elevator with me.

The elevator came to a jolting stop, snapping me from my thoughts. The doors opened filling the small metal cage with loud voices. A woman about five foot eight with dark brown hair pulled back into a ponytail stopped just outside the elevator doors. She peered over her shoulder back at me.

"Is everything all right, Dear?" she asked.

I always liked British accents. The way they pronounce their letters differently from ours. My eyes began to moisten from her question. A woman I never even met before knew something was wrong with me, but how?

I nodded before finally speaking. "Um, yeah. I'm fine," I choked back the tears threatening to escape.

"Are you sure?" She took a step toward the elevator doors, placing a hand out just as the doors began to close.

What was this woman's problem? Didn't she know I didn't want to talk. "I'm sure," I replied, stepping forward and walking through the open doors. The woman moved aside, allowing me to brush past her. No other words were spoken, although I could feel her gaze following me as I hurried through the lobby.

I made my way down the long hall toward the restaurant. My mom sat at a table in the far corner. My insides melted when I noticed her alone, feeling relieved. Where was my dad and brother? I should be excited that he wasn't there but found myself searching the room for him.

"Hey, there you are," mom smiled.

I pulled out a chair and sat across from her.

"I wasn't sure if I needed to go back up to the room and get you."

My eyes squinted at her, unsure of what she meant. "Why would you need to come up to the room?" *Had it been her that I had heard?*

Her eyes narrowed. "Um," she said, shaking her head. "To check on you, of course."

I nodded, relief flowing through me.

"Believe it or not Mia, you're my daughter and I love and worry about you."

My heart swelled, soaking in her words. I was afraid to reply to her, in fear of crying.

She took a drink from her glass then set it back down. "I was talking to your father, and we decided that he and Ethan would do something together. There's a town a few miles away. I thought we would…"

"We would what? Spend the day together?" The words came out harsh and out of nowhere.

"Mia!" Her voice rose, her eyes searching to see if anyone had heard. She leaned forward, lowering her voice. "I'm not sure what has gotten into you lately, but all I'm trying to do is spend some time with my daughter before she leaves for college next year."

I started to say, *'I'm sorry'*, but the words were trapped in my throat. Maybe it wouldn't be a bad idea, but I hoped she didn't think it would make up for all the times she hadn't spent with me. "It does sound nice," I replied. The napkin I had grabbed from the table was on my lap in pieces. I gathered the shredded pieces and hid them in the palm of my hand to throw them away.

"Do you want something to eat before we go?"

I shook my head. There was no way I could eat after last night. No way I could keep it down even if I tried.

"All right then, if you're ready so am I." She pushed her chair back and stood, brushing the front of her skirt.

∼

Twenty or so minutes later, we arrived in a small town. It looked like one of those hallmark movies where the buildings were attached side-by-side. Each was a different color with their own display in the window.

"Let's start here and walk down this side of the street then come up the other side," my mom said. "What do you think, Mia?"

"Sure, that sounds good." I really didn't care what we did as long as we stayed clear of my brother.

My mom led the way, stopping at the first display window we came to. There were mannequins dressed in children's clothes. We had no small children in our family, so we kept walking. The next store had all different kinds of knick-knacks in the window.

"Ah, now this store looks inviting," my mom said, stepping toward the door.

A bell *jingled* as we walked inside. There were knicks-knacks all along the walls and on shelves. I strolled through the store looking for something to take home to Trevor. I had already gotten him a T-shirt from the gift store in the lobby of our hotel. I wanted to get him something more special than just the T-shirt.

Strolling down the aisle, I stopped at a display filled with figurines holding a football. One figurine had its arm extended getting ready to throw the football. It was the perfect gift for Trevor. My eyes scanned the room, looking for someone who worked here. I spotted a man near the counter and waved my hand.

"How can I help you?" he asked. He had a genuine smile that filled his face.

"Hi, I'd like to purchase this item," I replied, pointing to the figurine with its arm extended.

"Aww, you must know a football player."

I smiled. "Yeah, my boyfriend back home plays football and was just accepted into UCLA next fall," I beamed with excitement.

"Then I think this will be a lovely gift for him." The male clerk reached into his side pocket and brought out a pair of keys and unlocked the display cabinet.

"I'm going to keep shopping if that's okay," I said.

"Of course, of course, I'll just put this behind the counter for you when you're ready to check out."

Nodding, I continued down the aisle. My mom stood a few feet in front of me. She was staring at something on the wall. I came up beside her and looked to where she was gazing. It was a portrait of a family on the beach.

"Isn't it beautiful?" my mom whispered.

"A picture of strangers," I replied.

She laughed. "That is sort of funny. No, it gave me an idea. I want a portrait of our family just like this one."

My eyes scanned the picture. They looked like a happy family and wondered if they had secrets like we did. "Yeah, it's umm, nice," I replied and stepped around her, browsing the shelves. I knew right then that I could never tell her what Ethan did to me last night.

Thirty-Five
Judith

By the time we drove back toward the hotel, the sun was descending. I didn't want our day to end. We had laughed and window shopped, eating ice cream as we walked. For the first time in a long time, we hadn't fought. In fact, Mia was polite and pleasant, which made me wonder if she was pretending to have a good time, but I didn't want to read too much into anything. I wanted to enjoy what time we had together before meeting the guys for dinner.

Pulling up to the entrance, I opened the door and climbed out. Mia stood on the sidewalk, waiting. Her eyes scanned the scenery. Was she looking for someone? The only people she knew were Scott and Ethan.

"Hey," I said. "Everything okay?" I reached out my hand and touched her shoulder. Mia's body jerked. Had I startled her? She turned toward me. Her eyes were wide with fright, then softened when she saw that it was me. Before I could say anything, she turned and hurried away. Clearly something was going on with her. Had I said something to upset her? I didn't think so. Then a trickle of a thought passed through my mind. Had someone hurt Mia? She had jumped from my touch as if scared, frightened of someone or something.

Mia skittered down the path heading toward the beach. My daughter needed me, so I hurried after her. Hot sand sprayed across my feet. The sandals I had on made it hard to catch up to her. I went to slip the sandals from my feet when through my peripheral vision Mia halted and spun around.

"Mom, could you please not follow me!" she hollered.

Frozen in my spot, I looked around, but no one was paying any attention to us. I went to speak, but Mia twisted back around and ran toward the shore, leaving me standing by myself. Her voice sounded on the verge of tears. What had I done to make her cry and not want to talk to me?

I wanted so much to chase after her but at the same time I didn't want to push. We already had a strained relationship, and I didn't want to make it worse by forcing myself onto her. I wanted her to come to me but I knew that was never going to happen.

"Judith."

Spinning around, I looked for the person who had called my name and spotted Scott across the driveway, waving at me. I scurried up the walk toward him. He jogged to meet me halfway.

"Hey, how was your day with Mia?" he asked, skimming the area.

I smiled. "It was good." It wasn't a total lie. We did have a good time until, well, until a minute ago. "How about you and Ethan?" I searched the landscape looking for my son but didn't see him.

"It was great! After we rode the jet skis, we rented ATV's and rode through the mountains and saw some wildlife. I wish you could have been there Jud. We came across this waterfall that you would never know existed."

He continued talking but my mind was still on Mia. Eventually, I chimed in. "That sounds amazing." But I didn't know what he was talking about.

"Where's Mia?" he asked, searching the scenery.

I glanced over my right shoulder toward the ocean. "She decided to go for a walk on the beach."

"You didn't have another one of your fights, did you?"

He was bringing this up now. Besides, why did he think we did nothing but fight? I shook my head. "No, we actually had a great time in town," I smiled, my mind retracing over the past few hours.

"Really?"

"Don't seem so surprised Scott. Mia and I can get along, you know." I crossed my arms in front of me. He didn't think Mia and I could be civil with one another?

Rubbing a hand down my arm; his way of consoling me. "I didn't mean it like that, Jud."

I nodded. "I'm sorry. I shouldn't have snapped at you."

He enveloped me in his arms, holding me tight.

"Where's Ethan?" I asked.

"He went for a walk on the beach too."

Thirty-Six
Mia

The hot sand smoothed my achy feet from walking all day in town. I should have known better to not to wear sandals, but when you're in a place like this, it doesn't make sense to wear anything but sandals.

My ears perked to the sound of waves rolling onto the shore and then back out to sea. For a tiny millimeter of a second, I wished the sea would take me with it. Scooping me up and washing me away out to sea and away from my family. When the next wave rolled ashore, I moved toward the water. The water covered my feet, leaving them cool, yet sticky with saltwater.

Turning, I walked a few feet up the beach, away from the water and plopped down onto the sand, facing the amazing view of the ocean. For the first time in a long time, I had a great time with my mom. We didn't talk much but it was nice to just being together. Though I won't ever tell her that. I wouldn't want her to think that we have made up and can be like we once were.

My mind whirled back in time to when my mom and I had started feuding. She had been working long hours and I needed her. I needed her to be there for me as the teenage years began to change me into a woman. Things with Trevor and our relationship. Things I didn't understand, though I had my best friend Kat until I didn't. But Kat didn't understand things either and her mom had just started feeling sick, so I didn't want to bother her with my problems. My mom seemed to never have time for me, but always made time for Ethan.

A shiver ran through my body at the thought of his name. To be honest, I was doing fine until we arrived back at the hotel. I had searched for Ethan but hadn't seen him. Though it was all a matter of time before I did, then what? I wasn't sure how I was going to act around him. If it were my choice, I'd hide out in my room until the day we left this place. A place I planned never to visit again, thanks to my brother.

My body stiffened. You know how sometimes you feel someone might be watching you? This was one of those times. Turning my neck, I glanced over my shoulder. In the distance, my brother was leaning against a palm tree. His arms were crossed in front of his chest. Jumping to my feet, I stumbled backward nearly falling onto my ass. I turned and ran toward the hotel. I wanted nothing more than to get to my room and lock the door. Only then would I feel safe again.

~

Finally, the last several days flew by and we landed back in Ohio, heading toward home. Trevor was sitting on our front porch when we pulled into the driveway. The moment my dad parked the car, I thrust open the passenger door and bolted out. Trevor stood, making his way to me. I ran into his open arms, and he wrapped me in a tight embrace, twirling me around. I couldn't help but giggle at his happiness to see me.

"I missed you so much," he said.

I kissed him. "I missed you too."

"Mia, come help with the bags," my dad hollered.

"Dad, we just got home!" I yelled.

"Here, let me help you Mr. Barnes," Trevor said, letting me go and sprinting over to the car.

"I've told you, son, to call me Scott."

"Sorry," Trevor replied, lifting a suitcase from the trunk.

Ethan stood behind my dad, staring directly at me. My insides quivered and I looked away, my stomach stirring. After what had happened in the Bahamas, I vowed not to tell Trevor what Ethan had done. I hadn't even told my parents what had happened. Would they be upset with him? Or with me? But I didn't do anything wrong, did I? Now I was questioning myself. Had the clothes I'd worn been too revealing? I started to shake my head when I glanced back in the direction of the car. My brother was still staring at me, but I was his sister. My stomach plummeted, trembling with nausea. I swallowed and dropped my eyes to the ground.

"Hey, everything okay?" Trevor asked, walking up beside me, placing a hand on my arm.

I jerked away. The bruises on my arms were tender to the touch. My eyes darted up, looking into Trevor's eyes. His eyebrows wrinkled, looking concerned. Thankful I had worn long sleeves so no one would see the bruises, which were now a deep purple.

"Sorry," I said, throwing a smile on my face for reassurance. "I'm fine. Really, I am." But that was an absolute lie. I glanced back toward my dad, but Ethan wasn't there. My shoulders relaxed. I headed toward the car and grabbed the rest of our stuff.

Trevor stayed for most of the evening. After helping me put my things away, we cuddled together on the swing on the front porch until it got dark. I walked with him to his car. We kissed and he held me in his arms which felt like heaven, not that I know what heaven feels like.

"Are you okay, Mia?" Trevor asked. "You seem different now that you're home. Almost like you're somewhere else."

I placed my head on his chest, wanting so much to tell him what had happened, but I couldn't. I was sure it was a fluke, and my brother didn't mean to do what he did, even though he was still acting weird around me. Still watching me.

"I'm fine now that I'm home and with you."

"I missed you so much," Trevor whispered into my ear, sending tingles down my spine.

"I missed you too. Will I see you tomorrow?"

"Um, I have a few jobs during the day, but I can come over afterward."

"I'd liked that."

Minutes later, I climbed the steps and went inside. My parents were sitting in the living room watching some show I hadn't seen before. They were laughing as they held one another. My dad turned and looked at me.

"Hey, Mia. Come sit." He padded the cushion next to him.

I shook my head. "I'm going to my room. I'm tired from the flight."

He nodded before turning back toward the TV. His laughter traveled down the hall. I climbed the stairs, hesitating at the landing, taking gentle steps, not wanting to make a sound by stepping on any loose floorboards. Ethan's door remained closed as I hurried past his door.

Once in my room, I closed and locked the door. I pressed my back against the wood, releasing the air in my lungs. Why did I feel scared of my brother? He wouldn't do anything to hurt me, but that thought vanished, recalling the events that happened a few days ago. Something was definitely going on with him. I just didn't know what.

Thirty-Seven
Mia

A couple weeks had gone by without any confrontation with my brother. In fact, he had left for college, which was even better. I could finally let my guard down. Whatever Ethan was going through when we were in the Bahamas had ended. A mistake and nothing more.

Trevor and I were heading to the lake for the Fourth of July weekend. We had just left the grocery store five miles from a cabin we reserved for the weekend with four of our closest friends. It took some persuading, but my parents relented, and added, *"make good choices, Mia"*.

For the first time since the trip to the Bahamas, I felt relaxed and grateful to get away. Although on occasion my mind would go back to the trip. The long stares Ethan had given me when we were in the same room together. His presence made me shiver with fear the more I was around him, wishing I had someone to talk to about what had happened. I thought about telling Trevor, but would he believe me? There was no way I would lie about my brother kissing me. It was like he was obsessed with me, but that would be gross and weird no matter how you looked at it.

I stared at Trevor while he drove. He had one hand on the wheel and the other lying on the open window. We drove down the gravel road toward the cabin. The warm summer air blowing his hair. We had just passed the sign to the entrance. There was a line of cars in front of us, not many, maybe eight to ten. We came to a stop; Trevor reached over and squeezed my hand.

"Mia, your hands are freezing," he said, rubbing his calloused hand over the top of mine, then picked up my hand and brought it to his lips, blowing his warm breath on them.

Tingles gushed through my body. I squirmed in my seat, shaking the feeling away even though it was a good feeling. His laugh bounced around the car, making me giggle. God, I loved him. He was an amazing boyfriend. One I was beyond thankful to have found.

The town of Crawford wasn't huge in population but there were plenty of guys to choose from but no one nearly as handsome and smart as Trevor. He was a one-of-a-kind guy, and I was blessed to have him all to myself. I had my eye on Trevor the moment he entered my biology class in the tenth grade. And as you would know it, the teacher had him sit right next to me. We had been together ever since.

I looked over at him, smiling. "I love you, Trev."

"I love you too." He reached over and kissed me. I sank into him not wanting the moment to end.

~

The sky lit up with blue, red, and white colors shooting in every direction. It was breathtaking. Watching fireworks made me feel like a child all over again. It never got old, but what made it more perfect was having Trevor right next to me, holding me in his arms. We laid on the blanket, looking up at the night sky. I felt safe with him.

He was my person.

My whole world.

I don't know what I'd ever do without him.

Our two friends and their significant others were lying on a blanket a few feet away. Their laughter made me turn and look at them. But there was something else I spotted. In the distance, along the wood line, there stood a familiar face.

The sky lit up with bright colors then went dark. Had I really seen him standing there? It couldn't be possible. I hadn't known he was planning on coming here this weekend too or I would have changed our plans even though Trevor and I had made them last year because the cabins rented out fast.

Another flash of light lit up the sky. I continued to stare at the same spot. Yes, it was him. It was my brother Ethan. He stood leaning beside a tree, his arms folded across his chest, staring right at me just like he did on the beach.

My body stiffened.

"Mia, what's wrong?" Trevor asked.

The sky went dark then lit up again, but this time he was gone. I looked all around not seeing him anywhere.

"Mia?"

I snapped to attention, turning toward Trevor.

"Are you okay?"

"Yeah, I'm fine." Even though I wasn't. I hated lying to him, but I didn't know how to tell him about the Bahamas or what I just saw.

Thirty-Eight
Judith

It didn't take long for me to get back into the swing of things after being on vacation. One that I had needed for a long time. I also hadn't realized how much I was working every day. The hours added up, leaving less time for my family. The family I loved more than anything and would do anything for. Maybe I should pull back? Spend more time with Mia before she leaves next year. I could plan a spa day together. Get our nails done and a full body massage. A smile played on my lips. Yes, I would make the appointments for us.

Inserting the key into the lock of my office door, I turned the knob and opened the door. Sunlight beamed in through the blind hanging on the window, cascading fragments of light across my desk. Dust particles danced in the air.

I walked across the room to my desk and pulled out the bottom drawer. Placing my purse inside, I shut it with my foot before sitting in the plush leather chair. The briefcase sat on my lap as I reached inside for my laptop.

My fingers moved across the keys, tapping in my password. The screen changed to the photo we had taken on the beach just a couple weeks ago. After finding a photographer who took pictures of us on the beach, just like the portrait I had seen in the store.

My body jumped at the loud knock on my office door. I looked up as it opened. Jackie, my receptionist, stuck her head inside.

"Good morning, do you have a minute?" Jackie said.

I closed the laptop, giving her my full attention. "Yes, of course, come in, come in," I replied, motioning my hand toward the chair in front of my desk.

Jackie sat in the leather chair, holding a paper in her hand. She seemed occupied, nervous even.

"What can I help you with?" She bit her lip before swallowing and making eye contact, only to look away again.

"Jackie, is everything all right?" I leaned forward, turning my ear in her direction. Her voice was low, whisper-like. She handed me a paper. "What's this?" I peered down at the paper now in my hand, focusing on the words.

"I, um…I'm giving you…."

"Two weeks' notice?" I interrupted.

She nodded. "I'm sorry but my father is very sick, and I need to take care of him."

"Doesn't he live in Florida?"

"Yes, I'm moving there to help take care of him; he doesn't have the money to go into one of those assisted living homes."

"Oh," I sat back against the chair, digesting her words. "I'm so sorry to hear about your father and to be losing you. You've been such a wonderful receptionist." To be honest she was the best one I had in a very long time, and I will be sad to see her go. "No chance he could move up here and live with you?"

She shook her head. "He loves his home. It belongs to him and my mom, God rest her soul."

"I understand."

"I also took the initiative and placed an AD online and in the newspaper for a replacement. I know how busy you are lately and knew you wouldn't have time."

I told you she was the best. "Thank you for that. I do appreciate everything you do for me and have done. If you'd like I can type up a reference for you? I'm sure you will need a job there."

"That would be amazing." Her cheeks turned rosy. A wide grin spread across her face.

"Anything I can do to help. I'll have it done before you leave." I smiled, hiding the disappointment growing inside me.

She stood and stepped away from the chair just as the phone rang in the other room. "I should get that," she said and hurried away, closing the door behind her.

I was still processing Jackie's words. I didn't want to lose her, but I couldn't make her stay. How would I ever find someone as good as her?

~

I had seen four patients today and was finishing up the notes on the computer when there was a knock on my door. Looking at my watch, I realized it was past five. I waited for the door to open and for my receptionist to poke her head inside. Which she always did when she was leaving for the night, but the door didn't open.

There was another knock on the door. "Come in," I hollered. When no one came in, I stood and made my way to the door. The lip of the rug was creased just enough that my heel caught the edge making me fall forward onto the chair several feet from the door.

"Shit," I swore. Pain shot through my foot. The foot I just twisted on the stupid shag carpet. I had been meaning to throw out the rug because of this reason. I didn't want any of my patients to trip and fall.

Standing upright, I put weight on my foot and winced. Pain shot up my leg. I squeezed my eyes shut when the knock came again. *They were persistent, weren't they?*

"One moment please," I hollered, limping to the door. I wrapped my hand around the knob and turned. A young woman stood in front of me. She had long, slender legs like toothpicks.

Her long blonde hair draped over her shoulders. She wore an oversized tan sweater and a necklace with a heart dangling from a silver chain.

"Hi, uh... my name is Olivia," the young woman said.

I stared at her, waiting for more.

"I, uh... I saw the AD online for the receptionist position."

That was fast. "Oh, yes the AD."

"You did place an AD online for a receptionist position, didn't you?"

I nodded. "Yes, well actually my receptionist did."

Her forehead creased.

"I'm sorry, come in and take a seat," I replied.

"Are you sure. I mean if this isn't a good time, I can come back."

"No, no. It's fine." I stepped back, holding the door open for her to come inside. "Have a seat and I'll do an interview with you." Once she was inside, I closed the door behind her. I made my way to the chair across the room, flinching at the pain.

"Are you all right? You look as if..."

I cut her off. "I'm fine, just twisted my ankle."

"Oh, are you sure it's a good time?"

"Yes. I'm sorry, what did you say your name was again?"

"Olivia. Olivia Blake."

"Nice to meet you, Olivia. My name is Judith Barnes, I'm one of the psychiatrists here in the building. You said you're applying for the receptionist job?"

"Yes, that's right."

"Do you have any past experience as a receptionist?" Olivia handed me several papers I hadn't noticed she was holding. I scanned over the resume, looking over her past jobs and skills.

"I worked at a church in Willow, helping with clerical work and at a doctor's office a couple times a week," she stated.

Smiling and nodding, Willow was a couple towns over. I thumbed through the papers, spotting a page with three references. All three stated how amazing it was to work with Olivia and recommend her for any job she applied for. "Are you not from this area?"

"I actually just moved to Crawford a week ago. I was online looking at several different jobs when I spotted this one."

Fifteen minutes later I stood. "I'll look these over and give you a call in a few days."

She rose from the chair. "Wonderful, I'll be waiting for your call. You won't have to worry about a thing. I'm very dependable and will have no issues getting whatever you need done asap."

Tilting my head, she seemed confident, yet needy. "I'm sure you will," I replied.

She stepped around the chair and walked to the door. "My cell number is listed at the top for you."

"Thank you, I'll get back to you as soon as possible. If you're considered for the position, you'll be my secretary and I'll have you come in and shadow my receptionist to see how things are done."

"That would be wonderful. Thank you so much!" Olivia opened the door and stepped out into the hall, closing it behind her.

I fell back onto the chair, exhaling the breath I had been holding. The pain in my foot was killing me. After a few minutes, I stood and limped to my desk. I packed my things and left the office.

Thirty-Nine
Mia

Days slipped away, but not the feeling of my brother watching my every move. Why was he doing this? I was his sister of all people. He shouldn't be trying to kiss me. Brothers don't do that shit! Brothers don't stalk their siblings, do they? Surely, I can't be the only person in the world going through this, can I? Brothers obsessing over their sisters. No, that certainly would be wrong in every aspect.

I rolled over and grabbed my cell phone lying face down on the nightstand. There was a text from Trevor. I opened it.

Trevor: "Hey babe, just wanted to say good morning and that I love you."

A smile crept on my face, making me feel almost one hundred percent better than I had just a few seconds ago.

Me: "Good morning. Love you too."

I let out a sigh before flipping onto my back not wanting to get up. I couldn't stay in bed all day, even though it was summer. Besides, I didn't have anything else to do today.

Staring up at the ceiling, I decided I needed to get up and do something productive. I threw the blankets to the side and slipped out of bed. After using the toilet, I stood at the sink looking in the mirror. I hadn't noticed when I came into the bathroom. There were words scribbled on the mirror with black eyeliner.

I'm watching you.

My heart pounded. He had come into my room last night when I was sleeping. Had he done it before? If so, how long had he been coming into my room without me knowing?

I grabbed the glass on the counter and filled it with water. Bitter acid entered my mouth. I swallowed hoping to wash away the taste. The thought of him in my room repulsed me. I would have to make sure my bedroom door was always locked, but would that keep him out? He could have a key. He could unlock the door. Which meant he could come into my room anytime he wanted. I wouldn't be able to sleep knowing he was coming into my room. I wouldn't feel safe until he left for college.

I grabbed some toilet paper and wiped the words off the mirror, but not before I took a picture. I needed to make sure I kept proof of what he was doing to me. Tossing the toilet paper into the wastebasket, I then lifted the toilet seat and spewed the contents from my stomach.

~

Racing down the hall toward the stairs, the hood of my jacket was smacking against my back. With my left hand, I grasped the wooden rail and raced up the staircase. My heart was thrashing beneath the concert T-shirt I had bought months ago. Glancing over my shoulder, I tripped. My knee smacked the hard wood, sending a sharp sting of pain up my leg.

"Fuck," I cried through gritted teeth.

Closing my eyes, I pushed the pain from my mind. I didn't have time to stop. Didn't have time to console myself like a child needing her mommy to kiss the hurt away. Not that I recalled my mom ever doing such a thing with me.

My grip tightened around the railing, my fingernails digging into the wood, limping the rest of the way to the top. Peering over my shoulder again, but I saw no one. Then the floorboard creaked beneath his weight. He was coming for me, and I had nowhere to hide but my bedroom which seemed too far to reach. What other choice did I have? I needed to get to my room and lock the fucking door!

Grabbing the banister, I pushed myself forward and around the railing at the top of the stairs. I sprinted down the hall, my knee screaming out obscenities like a Robin Williams comedy show, though I wasn't laughing. The only thought racing through my mind was getting inside my bedroom before he could get me.

Extending my arm, the skin of my palm brushed against the cold metal knob. Before I could grip the handle and throw the door open, my body was yanked back away from the door. The security of my bedroom was getting further and further away. I kicked and screamed with everything I had in me. His arm clamped around my mid-section and the other hand was over my mouth to silence me, not that there was anyone here to hear me scream.

My stomach clenched as I stifled a cry.

It was no use.

He was stronger than me.

I felt his hot, sticky breath against my neck as he dragged me down the hall to his bedroom.

Part Four

*Together we will rebuild what is damaged
and in return it will make us stronger...*

Quote by Donna M. Zadunajsky

Judith and Mia
Now

Forty
Mia

Sitting in the backseat, I stared out the window. My eyes scanned over the homes, watching children play in the yard. Neither of my parents said a word since we got in the car. Finding words was hard sometimes. I get it, I do, but they haven't seen me in three weeks. Don't they want to know how I am? How my stay was in that place? I allowed myself to laugh at the last thought. It wasn't like I had been away at some resort or summer camp. Or maybe they weren't sure what to talk about. Did they know what happened to my friend Aiden? I'm sure Dr. Harding wouldn't have told them about our sessions. They were confidential, weren't they? I wasn't an adult yet. Just a few months to go. But wouldn't that be breaking doctor/patient confidentiality?

"Mia, we're almost home," my dad said from the driver's seat.

My eyes shifted toward the rear-view mirror, giving a small nod in return. I searched the scenery for Trevor's car. I didn't see it, and my insides melted with relief. I wasn't ready to see him or to talk to him about what I'd done. I could never tell him what happened to me. I couldn't allow the words to flutter off my tongue, knowing he wouldn't understand. Knowing he would feel repulsed and wouldn't want me any longer.

The blinker sounded throughout the car, letting me know we were pulling into the driveway. I let out the breath I was holding. This was it. There would be nowhere for me to go once I entered the house. My parents, I was sure, were waiting until we arrived home to talk about what had happened. I wasn't ready to talk. I wasn't ready to let anyone know what transpired and why I did it. They would just have to accept my decision and allow me to come to them, but that wasn't going to ever happen. The idea of talking about what I did and why, was sending a panic through my body.

We parked inside the garage. I swallowed then opened the door, placing one foot out then the other. My insides stirred. All I wanted to do was climb back inside the car and shut the door. I didn't think I can go inside.

"Mia," my mom said. "Are you all right? You look white as a ghost."

I felt a hand wrap around my arm, and I quickly jerked away. My body hit the car door, a muffled cry leaving my lips. A tingling pain shot from my elbow to my hand. I closed my eyes, waiting for the pain to dissipate.

"Mia let me help you inside," my dad said beside me.

I nodded, allowing him to place an arm around me. Once inside, my eyes scanned the kitchen. No one was there. It was only the three of us. I hadn't seen his car parked at the curb, which meant he must be at college. Relief rained over me.

"I'm feeling kind of tired," I whispered, shifting my eyes from my mom to my dad.

"Oh, all right," mom said. "I guess we will talk later once you've gotten some rest." Her face fell.

"Are you hungry? Do you want something to eat before you lay down?" dad asked.

I shook my head. "I'm fine. I'm good. Just tired. I didn't sleep well last night." My eyes swept over their faces again before I turned away, heading toward the stairs. I couldn't look at them or be in the same room with them. They made me feel more depressed. Their sad and disappointing stares. I gave a half-clenched smile as I turned away, heading toward the stairs.

"I'll come with you," my mom said. "Just to make sure you don't faint. You still look like you've seen a ghost."

I was about to say something to her. To tell her I didn't need her to baby me, but the truth was, I did need my mom. I needed her more than anything, but I couldn't tell her that. With a nod of my head, she followed behind me and up the stairs. My eyes darted to Ethan's closed bedroom door, my heart racing. A hand touched my arm, making me jerk away.

"Mia?"

I hurried down the hall to my room, my mom's footsteps right behind me. Opening the door, I scanned the room. Relief swept over me as I peered inside. Was I expecting to find someone inside my room?

"Mia, sweetie, are you okay?"

Her voice whispered in my ear, then a light touch of her hand on my shoulder. I turned toward her and fell into her arms. She wrapped me into an embrace and for the first time in weeks I felt safe.

Forty-One
Judith

Once I stepped outside my daughter's bedroom, I scurried down the hall to my room. I closed the door, pressing my back against it. The tightness in my chest clenched and unclenched. Another panic attack wasn't what I needed at this moment. When the pressure released, I took in a deep much needed breath. The feel of my daughter and the softness of her hair melted my heart. She had let me hold her. For the first time in a very long time, we hugged like our lives depended on it.

I closed my eyes, letting the air escape through my parted lips. I needed to stop this. I was stronger than I was allowing myself to be at this moment. What was happening to me lately? I wasn't this person that was standing here, hiding behind a closed door, shielding myself from people and life. I was a person who helped others, and now I was the one who needed help.

The door to the bathroom opened making me jump. I had thought I was alone in the room.

"Hey, what are you doing?" Scott asked, standing in the doorway wearing only a towel. Water dripped from his hair and ran down his back and along his muscular chest.

What must he think of me being so susceptible? My body was pressed against the door as if I were trying to keep someone or something out. I was scared like a child afraid of the boogeyman.

"Hi," I finally replied, adding a smile. *Don't let him see you crumble.*

"Everything okay?" his brows creased. "Is Mia…?"

"Mia is fine." Now I was scaring him. I had to come up with something quick before he asked more questions. I reached behind me for the knob and locked it, keeping my eyes on him the whole time. He looked so gorgeous standing there. I was turned on by his appearance. It had been since our trip that we have had sex. I had been consumed by the things that have led me to this very place. *Forget about what happened for only a moment. Let yourself feel. Let yourself live Judith.*

Gliding toward him, I stood in front of him. Reaching my hand out, I loosened the towel, letting it drop to the floor. I missed this so much. He brushed his hand against my face and felt the softness of his skin on mine. He lowered his head and kissed me ever so gently. Everything that had clogged my mind lately had slipped away.

~

I stood in the kitchen preparing dinner, a smile pasted on my face. The lovemaking had been mind-blowing and something I had missed since our vacation. Too consumed with my own feelings I had neglected his. Scott was an amazing husband and father, and I was grateful to have met him back in college.

It had taken some coercing, but my roommate and her friends had talked me into going to a party. I wasn't like the other girls. I came to college for the education, not too party, which seemed to be all my roommate did with her time. Hell, half the campus spent all their time partying.

"Come with us. You'll have a good time, I promise," my roommate had persuaded.

"Yeah, like a really good time," one of the other girls said with a wink and a giggle.

I didn't know what was so funny about what the girl had said. Was she high or drunk? I didn't know if there was a difference between the two. I had never been high before. I guess I could break out of my shell and have some fun for a change or at least for tonight.

"Okay, fine," I had replied. "I'll go, but I can't promise I'll stay out all night."

Two of the four girls cackled and hooted.

Once at the party, I was handed a drink which tasted disgusting, but I sipped on it anyway. It didn't take long for a buzz to kick in and make my brain feel fuzzy. This wasn't my first alcoholic drink; I had been to quite a few high school parties in the past, I just didn't drink often.

My friends had already ditched me, so I made my way outside, while they danced in the living room and mingled with other college students. I scanned the crowd and there he was standing out by the pool talking to some guy dressed in a grass skirt. I wasn't sure why the guy was dressed that way. There was no theme as far as I could tell. No one else was wearing grass skirts.

The guy looked my way, and I glanced down at my feet. The next thing I knew, he was standing in front of me. We had talked all night and by the end of the following week, we were dating. I never regretted a single minute of that night or what happened next. One year and two weeks later we were married. In fact, I had thanked my roommate for pushing me to go out that night. Because I wouldn't have met Scott and lost out on our life together.

The smile spread wider across my face as I recalled the events of my youth which led me to where I was now. In the home that Scott and I had bought and where we had started a family.

"Hey, what's for dinner?"

The wine glass in my hand dropped to the floor, shattering into a million little pieces.

Forty-Two

Mia

My cell phone was on the nightstand, so I grabbed it and turned it on. I pondered as it rebooted, just how many text messages and voicemails were waiting for me?

Seconds later, my phone lit up. Notifications flicked across the screen one right after another. Just how many messages did I have? Trevor's name appeared a zillion times and I wondered if I had made the right choice not to contact him. Did he even know I was home? Had my parents talked to him about what had happened?

What did he say?

How did he feel?

What did he think of me?

So many questions crossed my mind, but the only way for me to find out was to read every single text he had sent me.

Glass shattered below me. Leaping off my bed, I rushed to the door. Pressing my ear against the wood, listening for what, I wasn't sure. I could only hear my heartbeat pulsating.

Outside in the hall, my dad's voice was loud. His footfalls pounding on the wooden steps as he hurried down the stairs to see what was going on. Maybe I should go see what had happened too? It could be bad. Wrapping my hand around the knob, I slowly turned the handle and poked my head out. The hall was empty. Not that I was expecting someone to be standing there in front of my door. Ethan wasn't here, and both of my parents were downstairs.

I tiptoed out into the hall and stood by the railing. Peering over the banister I didn't see anything or anyone. Should I dare go see what was going on or should I stay up here where I felt safe? Who am I kidding, I haven't felt safe in this house since what happened.

Taking small steps, I now stood on the landing looking down. The opening of the kitchen doorway appeared in my view, but no one was there.

"What happened in here?" my dad asked.

"Nothing. I…I accidentally dropped my wine glass," mom replied.

"I startled her," Ethan said.

My body stiffened.

The hair on my arms stood up. A chill ran through my body and my stomach plummeted. Just the sound of his voice made me cringe. The back of a foot appeared, then a leg. My dad's leg. He stepped back like he was about to leave the room. I made my way down the stairs but stopped a few steps before reaching the bottom. My dad was in the doorway facing the sink, which was probably where my mom stood. The sound of broken glass being swept up filled the silence, then nothing until the glass was dumped into the garbage can.

The wood creaked under my foot as I took another step. My head sprung up. My eyes now focused on my dad. He hadn't turned around, so I took a step back, making my way back up the stairs. Quietly, I hurried down the hall to my room, locking the door the moment I was back inside. I pressed my back against the door, my hand still on the doorknob.

Resting my head against the door, I closed my eyes. My heart was pounding.

"Breathe," I whispered.

Forty-Three
Judith

After cleaning up the mess I had made, I grabbed another glass from the cabinet and poured myself some more wine. I guzzled it down and poured another.

"Judith, slow down," Scott insisted. "What has gotten into you?"

With a shaky hand, I set the wine glass on the granite counter, nearly spilling the wine. "I didn't know you were home?" my voice cracked. *Why was I panicking? It was my son, not some intruder. But I knew why.*

"Thanks, I can feel the love in this room," Ethan replied, crossing his arms against his chest, and leaned against the counter.

"She didn't mean it like that," Scott said.

"My bad." Ethan emphasized. "I didn't know I had to let you know when I was coming home."

Would be nice if you did, I thought. "Just thought with school in session you wouldn't be able to come home until the weekends."

"Well, Dad told me Mia was coming home today so I wanted to see her. Welcome her home."

Why did he do that? I thought. *But Scott didn't know what I knew.* I wasn't sure when Scott appeared next to me, but I was thankful he had. His hand touched the small of my back, sending a wave of tingles up my spine. The lovemaking from minutes ago swam through me. "Yes, of course."

"Go upstairs and rest," Scott whispered in my ear, then kissed my head. "I'll finish dinner."

Had he felt me trembling beneath his touch? I nodded, grabbing the bottle of wine, and filling the glass to the rim. I'm not sure what came over me just now, but my son had to go. He couldn't be here. He wasn't welcome in this house, but Scott didn't know what I knew. The pictures of those girls were still etched in my mind. I mustered up everything I had left and scurried out of the kitchen without making eye contact with my son.

Once at the top of the stairs, I glanced down the hall toward Mia's room. Her door was closed, but that wasn't anything new. Even before the attempted suicide she had always kept her bedroom door closed. I wanted to go to her. I wanted to hold her in my arms again and tell her that I loved her, but I couldn't. Afraid of her rejecting me, even though she hadn't earlier. What were the chances that she would allow me into her room, into her arms, again? Besides, she didn't know I knew her secret. *Go to her Judith,* my mind whispered.

My hand dropped to my side as the other hand lifted the glass of wine to my lips. The soft, smooth taste left my mouth dry after I swallowed. I took another drink and another, finishing the glass. The whole time, I stared at the white wooden door in front of me. The room Ethan slept in. My stomach stirred, thoughts bouncing in my head.

I turned and slipped inside my bedroom, closing the door behind me. Resting my back against the door before sliding to the floor. Pulling my knees in, I wrapped my arms around them, hugging them in close. The child in me was back inside the small, dark closet in the hallway of my childhood home. My father's favorite place to put me when I disobeyed his orders. Along with no food for days. He beat my mother but locked me away like some rabid animal. I hated feeling scared and never thought I'd ever feel that way again. *When had our perfect family fallen apart? How long had Ethan been taking pictures of naked girls? Then it occurred to me. Had he done something to Mia?*

The thought sickened me.

Tears began to well up in my eyes. If I allowed the tears to flow, I wouldn't be able to stop.

On my hands and knees, I crawled to the bathroom and slipped inside, closing the door behind me. Using the door handle, I pulled myself up to my feet and walked to the shower stall. Opening the glass door, I grasped the knob inside and turned on the water. My clothes fell to the floor as I quickly undressed.

Once under the hot, steaming water, the floodgates opened, and everything poured out of me.

Forty-Four

Mia

A couple weeks later, I stared in the mirror at the dark circles under my eyes. The color of my skin had turned colorless since I'd lost so much weight. My sunken cheekbones made my eyes look bigger. I hadn't slept well last night, but that was nothing new. I hadn't slept well since I came back home. Especially the nights Ethan was here.

Shuffling my bare feet across the wooden floor, I walked to the window and peered out. The next school break wouldn't be until November, and I wanted a break from school now. Though, we did have Monday off for Labor Day. I needed time away from all the whispers flooding the halls. My classmates talked about me behind my back, though not very well since I could hear them. They didn't even look at me the same way as before. Like I was some fragile porcelain doll ready to crack, though I was already shattered inside. They wanted to know why I did what I did. Of course, no one knew why. Only I knew the truth. The truth I wasn't ready to tell anyone. It would destroy lives, just as it had destroyed mine.

My bedroom window faced Kat's house. My once again best friend after I finally apologized for what I did three years ago that ended our friendship. She had seen me kiss a boy she liked, but the thing was he had kissed me and when I pushed him away, there she was watching the whole thing go down. She wouldn't let me explain what happened, which ripped our friendship apart. She finally knew the truth and forgave me.

The blinds in her bedroom were still closed. Kat had never been one to sleep in past eight, but her shades being closed didn't mean she was still sleeping. She could be up. I was sure she was up.

How had I made it three years without her? Well, I was sure Kat didn't know I was watching her all these years. Not in a stalking kind of way. I just wanted to make sure she was okay.

When Kat's mom died, I had wanted nothing more than to go to Kat and comfort her, but I could tell she just wanted to be left alone. I knew what it was like to want nothing to do with anyone; especially after what happened this past summer. Besides, we weren't friends when all that stuff happened.

Turning away from the window, I walked into the closet and slipped into a pair of sandals. I grabbed the sweater from the foot of the bed and opened my bedroom door.

"Where are you going?" my brother Ethan asked.

My heart jolted beneath my ribcage. "You scared the shit out of me." I stepped back into my room, the metal knob slipping from my hand. An image flashed in my mind of the last time I had seen my brother. I hadn't known he was coming home for the weekend. My parents hadn't said a word to me. Did they even know he was here? What the fuck was he doing here!? I couldn't handle it if… *I have to get out of this house!*

"What are you doing here?" I asked.

"Nice to see you too. Where are you off to?"

"Um, Kat's."

"Kat's?"

I nodded.

"Since when do you and *her* hang out? Thought you weren't friends?"

It felt like all the air in the room had evaporated. I swallowed, letting out a dry cough.

"You, okay? Not getting sick, are you?" Ethan's head tilted slightly to the left. "Maybe you should stay home."

Over my dead body! How could he stand there and pretend what happened, didn't happen? Twisting, I grabbed the glass of water from the nightstand and gulped it down. Water splashed out of the cup and onto the front of my shirt. "Damn it," I muttered under my breath, placing the glass back down on the nightstand.

"Slow down, guzzler," Ethan laughed. Stepping closer, he reached out his hand and began to pat the water into the fabric of my shirt.

"Don't touch me!" I shouted. *What the flying hell was he doing?* My reaction was slow at first, then I was in flight mode. My hand raised in the air, then came down, slapping his hand away. I zipped around him and fled down the hall, taking the steps two at a time. Sprinting to the front door as if we were playing, *catch me if you can*, a game we played all the time as kids, but we weren't kids anymore. And I wasn't playing his stupid games. I wasn't sticking around waiting for him to catch me. Or worse hurt me again.

Once outside, the front door to my back, I let out the breath I had been holding. Being inside the house felt congested at times. More so since I tried to kill myself. My mom looked at me with searching eyes, like she was trying to read my mind. I know she just wanted to help. Wanted me to talk to her but I just can't. Not yet. Maybe never.

The wood brushed against the skin of my knuckles as I knocked on Kat's front door, unaware I had crossed the street. That happened sometimes when I got lost inside my head. I ended up in places, forgetting how I got there.

Kat's dog Eva, a golden retriever, let out a bark from inside the house. I knocked again before looking over my shoulder. Her dad's car wasn't in the driveway, which told me what exactly? Was Kat ignoring me? Or maybe she was in the shower and didn't hear me knocking or Eva barking.

Reaching out my hand, I twisted the doorknob to confirm that it was indeed locked. I waited another second before deciding to go around to the back of the house and check the back door.

I climbed the wooden steps. The boards moaned under my weight. I was sure it had nothing at all to do with my weight of one-hundred and two pounds. The boards were just old and made sounds when you walked on them.

I stood and turned toward the door, reaching out to knock when the door flew open. Eva bounded past my legs and down the stairs, nearly knocking me over on her way.

"Whoa, girl," I said, catching my footing. I reached back and grabbed the railing but kept my eyes forward.

Kat's face seemed conflicted with emotions. Was she happy to see me? Or surprised that I had been standing at the back door? Had she known I had knocked on the front door? Now I was confused. Nonetheless, I still needed my friend now more than any other time.

Kat reached a hand to her ear, removing the ear pods from each ear.

That explained why she hadn't heard me. "Hi, Kat, can I come in?" Kat stepped aside. I hurried past her and into the kitchen, feeling safe and secure.

The air smelled of cookies. But not just any cookies, oatmeal raisin; our favorite. I swallowed, my mouth watering. I stepped back, reaching for the counter to get a cookie.

"Did you make these for me?" I smiled before taking a bite. The cookie was still warm and practically melted in my mouth. God, it tasted so good. My stomach growled.

"Yes, but I was going to bring them to you after they cooled."

I tilted my head, surprised by her reply. She baked these for me, and she was going to bring them to me? "Yeah, don't go to my house."

"Why?"

"You know my parents, they're so annoying." Though that wasn't the real reason.

Kat nodded as if she understood, then opened the door for Eva to come back inside. "Okay, then what do you want to do instead?"

~

"We'll need some paper to keep track of our scores," Jim said.

"Okay, I'll get some," I replied, jumping to my feet. We had invited Trevor and Jim over to play cards. Once school started back up, I couldn't keep myself away from Trevor. Although I had tried hard to let him go, Trevor and I were a couple again. I couldn't live the rest of my life without him. He just had this way of pulling me back to him. Like I said, we were each other's person. We talked but not about what happened to me. He said he wouldn't pressure me, but wanted to let me know that he was there for me when I was ready to talk.

"There's some blank paper on my desk in my bedroom we can use," Kat stated from beside Jim on the floor in the living room.

"Okay, I'll be right back." I skittered down the hall to her bedroom. It was nice to see Kat happy for a change. I mean, I expected her to be sad from losing her mom and all. She just deserved happiness for a change, and I'm so glad Jim made her happy.

Once in Kat's room, I flipped on the light and spotted the desk against the wall to my left. Right where it had been since middle school. I was with them the day Kat's parents bought the desk for her. Then a few days later, I had the same one in my room. We always got the same identical things as the other when we were younger. The same clothes, the same magazines, and the same bed spread.

I glanced around the room, noticing how organized and clean Kat was now. She hadn't always been that way. Growing up, she didn't care about anything and threw her clothes on the floor; clean or dirty. Her mom would get so mad at her.

"They're not dirty if you only try them on," Kat's mom had said. "I'll just rehang them. I don't care if you did wear them outside."

Was that the reason Kat had changed? We weren't friends when her mom got sick. My parents were talking in the kitchen about Mrs. Palmer and that she was diagnosed with stage four cancer and had only a few months to live. I felt bad for Kat. I wanted to tell her how sorry I was for her loss, but I just couldn't bring myself to do it.

Maybe if I had, things would have been different between us. Maybe things would have been different, period. Then I wouldn't have tried to kill myself, which had nothing to do with us not being friends. But maybe she would have changed my mind? Because when we were friends long ago, we told each other everything.

Shuffling my feet, I walked over to the desk, creating enough static electricity to fuel the entire neighborhood. I reached out my hand to grab the blank paper when my hand touched on the metal keyboard. An electric shock zipped up my arm and I yanked my hand away, knocking the plastic trays off the desk. They flew in the air along with whatever papers Kat had on them before landing on the carpeted floor with a soft clatter.

"Aw, shit," I muttered, looking over my shoulder.

No one appeared behind me, which meant they hadn't heard the ruckus, thanks to the carpet. Bending over, I picked up the trays and placed them back on the desk. Then, I gathered the papers scattered on the floor. I had no idea what tray the papers went on, so I arranged them into a neat pile and placed them on one of the trays. Once I was finished, I grabbed a blank piece of paper. I turned to leave the room when my eyes caught sight of something in the trash can.

I wasn't one to snoop in anyone's personal things, especially Kat's. But there was something familiar about the piece of paper placed on top of the garbage.

Bending over, I grasped the paper between my fingers and removed it from the garbage. My eyes blurred over the words until they came into view. It was a copy of the note I had found inside my locker on the second day of school.

But how?

How did Kat have a copy of it?

Had she written the note? No, I knew who had written it. I just…

"Hey, what's taking you so long?" Kat said, bursting through the open doorway and coming to a halt in front of me.

I looked up from the paper in my hand and gave her a cold hard stare. Kat's mouth opened. She was about to say something when I spoke first. "What the hell is this?" I snapped, holding the paper up for Kat to see.

"Mia, I can explain."

"Then explain."

"I was in the restroom stall when the note fell out of your backpack. You had just left the restroom. I picked it up and…"

"And what? Decided to read it?"

"Well, not exactly." Kat's posture stiffened under her red cotton sweater.

"Not exactly what, Kat? Obviously, you read the note because you made a copy of it."

She nodded. "Yes," she cleared her throat. "I read the note when I got home that day from school. I made a copy of it…"

"I can see that."

"The next day I put the original note in your locker."

"Classic, Kat," I muttered.

"What does that mean?"

"When are you ever going to mind your own *effing* business? This has nothing to do with you, but you can't help yourself, can you?"

"Mia, I'm sorry. I…"

"You what? You know what? Just forget it. I don't want to hear any more of your excuses," I hissed.

Kat stepped forward, placing a hand on my arm. "Look, I don't know who wrote the letter, but obviously you are bothered by it."

I jerked my arm from under her hand. "You think?" I growled. Why was I so angry at her? Well, because I didn't want her to know who wrote the note or what secret I was hiding from her. From everyone. Or was I more afraid of Kat finding out that I had lied to her? That the secret I had told her was a flat-out fib. Then our newfound friendship would be over once again.

"Everything okay in here?" Trevor asked from the doorway. "I heard shouting."

We both turned and looked in his direction. I folded the paper and stuffed it into my back pocket.

"Yeah, everything's fine," I said and walked out of the bedroom. "Let's go." I couldn't stay in Kat's house another minute.

It was past eleven when Trevor dropped me off. The lights were off in the house, so I climbed the trellis to my bedroom window.

Forty-Five
Judith

When I woke, the clock beside the bed read 11:15 p.m. Turning my head, I could see the shape of Scott beside me. I pushed the quilt aside and slipped out of bed, trying hard not to make any noise. The floorboard creaked under my weight. I glanced over my shoulder, but Scott didn't stir. He had always been a sound sleeper. The tension in my neck and upper back wilted when I rolled my shoulders back. I needed to relax and stop being so on edge, but I knew why I was. I had secrets hiding inside me. Secrets I wasn't ready to tell Scott, but I couldn't hold them inside forever.

Turning away from the bed, my eyes followed the small nightlight glowing next to the bathroom door, lighting my way. I padded to the bathroom and closed the door.

A few minutes later, I tiptoed out of the bathroom, peering over my shoulder once more to make sure I hadn't woken my husband. Curling my fingers around the knob, I turned and opened the door. Darkness stared back at me. I stepped out into the hall, closing the door behind me with a *click*. It took a few seconds before my eyes adjusted to the dark.

The house was stagnant as I stood there looking down the hall toward Mia's room. *At least tonight my daughter wasn't waking up screaming, though it was still early in the evening,* I thought. I wasn't aware if Scott heard her. He had never mentioned anything to me, nor had he come running like I had to her room to check on her. I wanted to comfort her, but every time I entered her room, she bit off my head for intruding. Hadn't she wanted me to hold her and tell her that it was just a dream? Just a nightmare? That everything would be okay? There was no bogeyman hiding in her closet or under the bed. Though, she was too old to believe in all that. She wasn't a child afraid of the dark like I once was.

I blinked, realizing that I was now standing in front of her bedroom door. I hadn't recalled walking toward Mia's room once again, oblivious to the things around me.

Cool air nipped at my toes from under the door. I had forgotten to put on my slippers, not wanting to wake Scott. I had a bad habit of scuffing my feet against the wood floor when I walked, especially in my slippers.

There it was again. Why did I feel a breeze coming from under the door? The window, I questioned? There was nowhere else the air could be coming from. It wasn't hot enough for the air conditioner to be running at night.

I placed my hand on the doorknob and turned, but it wouldn't move; it was locked. Why was the door locked? Horrible thoughts flooded my mind. My heart raced, the blood pulsing in my ear.

Please no! My mind screamed. *Not again.*

Stop it, Judith. She's fine, my brain repeated. I couldn't allow myself to think about that right now. In all honesty, I just wanted to forget what had happened, but I also knew that would never happen. The images were forever embedded in my head. Even I had bad dreams about that night.

Stretching my arm above me, I felt around for the key. When I found it, I clenched the spare key between my fingers, then with a shaky hand placed the key in the lock. I drew in a deep breath and rested my head against the door, whispering a prayer. "Please, please let her be alive."

My head jerked away from the door and my back stiffened.

I heard a noise.

There was a noise coming from inside the room. A noise that sounded like a window closing, which would explain the draft I felt on my feet. Which also meant Mia was awake, but why would she be closing the window? Maybe she had opened it earlier. Or had she snuck out and was now climbing back inside?

I turned the key and felt the release as the door unlocked. Twisting the knob, I pushed the door open. She stood by the window. The light from the moon lit up the room.

"Mom?" Mia questioned.

I swallowed, feeling relief swim through me. She was okay. My daughter was standing in the room, and she was alive. My knees began to buckle beneath me. My hand automatically reached for the doorframe to keep myself from falling.

Mia was in front of me, wrapping her arm around my midsection. "Mom, are you all right?" she asked.

My head bounced up and down. My daughter sounded worried about me. I couldn't ever remember her caring before. The notion warmed my heart. Then as if a light switch had flicked on, she changed.

"What are you doing in my room? I thought I locked the door. How did you get in?"

"I umm…" I pressed the key into the palm of my hand, hiding it from her view. "I came out to get some water and heard a noise," I lied. If I had wanted water, I would have gotten some from the sink in my bathroom.

"Well, you don't need to check on me all the time. I'm fine," she snapped. "I'm not going…" she let the words hang in the air.

"Kill yourself?" the words slipped off my tongue before I could stop them. The muscles in my throat suppressed the words I wanted to say to her. There was so much I wanted to say to her. I let out a dry cough before looking up and into her eyes.

"I'm going to bed," Mia murmured.

She yanked her hand away like my skin was on fire. She stepped back and walked toward the door of the closet, disappearing inside. That was my queue to go. My daughter didn't want me in her room. She didn't need her mom. Why had I said those words?

I stepped out into the hall and pulled the door closed, but I didn't move. I stood waiting for what, I didn't know. I wished we could be a mother and a daughter who talked. I had a few acquaintances who were friends with their daughters, and I pondered if we could or would be like that, but I didn't think it would be possible. No matter what I did or didn't do, Mia always found a way to demolish it. Making me feel like I'm the bad person, but all I wanted to do was be there for her.

Maybe I should just keep pushing. Eventually, Mia would fold, and we could talk about what had happened. I didn't know the whole truth, but I wanted to know. I wanted to know exactly why she wanted nothing more than to end her life. Her beautiful life.

Forty-Six

Mia

After my mom left the room, I reached into the back pocket of my jeans. I couldn't believe Kat knew. Well, she didn't know the truth, but she had to know something wasn't right. She had never mentioned anything to me since we started talking again. Maybe she was waiting for me to say something? Maybe the note had been hidden with the other papers. Out of sight, out of mind, and Kat had forgotten all about the note, which was possible. A lot had happened in the last few weeks.

She said the note had fallen out of my backpack in the restroom on the first day of school. Which means that it was placed in my bag before then, but when exactly? I tried to think back to the week before school, when I had returned home from the inpatient treatment facility, which told me he placed the note in my bag when I was getting treatment.

I pulled the paper out of my back pocket and re-read it.

Mia,

Do you think killing yourself is a way out? That you can escape me? You'll never get away from me. You're a smart girl, Mia. I know I can count on you to keep my secret. Our secret. Do you think you can just end your life because of this? I won't make it that easy for you. I need you. You need me. So, don't think about trying it again!

Just like before, the note made my stomach sour. I sprinted to the bathroom, lifting the toilet seat as the oatmeal raisin cookies I had devoured earlier came shooting out of my mouth. *How could…* I heaved again.

"Mia are you all, right?" my mom asked from the doorway. "I heard you gagging."

I moaned and spat the acidic taste out of my mouth. Then grabbed some toilet paper from the roll, wiping my mouth. My mom stood beside me, towering over me.

I wasn't sure how I felt my mom's touch when she wasn't actually touching me. Her hand hovered above my head. She moved her hand away, letting it fall to her side. She couldn't even bring herself to want to touch me. A touch I so badly wanted, didn't I? Did I disgust her that much? Did she hate me for what I did?

How long was she going to stand there looking down at me? Without talking?

My mom always had something to say. I wasn't a bad child. I got good grades. I didn't get into trouble like Ethan did. She never scolded him for his bad behavior. To be honest, he could probably get away with murder, which in some sense he already had.

I sat back on my heels, placing my hands in my lap like an obedient dog. My eyes stared at the porcelain toilet. Before I could reach forward to flush, my mom beat me to it. Nervousness swam through me, but not in a sick feeling kind of way. Besides, there was nothing left to throw up. The dull pain in my back had returned, which had been happening since I had lost weight.

Water splashed onto my arm, snapping me out of my thoughts. I wiped it away. A cup appeared beside me filled with water.

"Here, drink this," mom said.

Grabbing the glass, I took a gulp, swishing it around inside my mouth before spitting it in the toilet. With the second sip, I let the cool crisp water run down my parched throat, the gross aftertaste disappearing.

"What's this?" she asked, bending forward.

My eyes darted to the floor where the note laid face up. I quickly snatched it before she could see the words written on the paper.

"Mia?"

"Mom, it's nothing, okay. Just leave it alone!" I snapped, not meaning to sound harsh. She stood there for another second before sitting on the edge of the tub. I was sure she was going to leave the room, but she didn't.

"Mia, no matter what you're going through I want you to know I'm here for you. You can tell me anything. I won't judge. I don't even have to talk. I'll only listen, you have my word."

My eyes began to water, and I sniffled. Her hand touched my back and before I knew it, she was on the floor holding me in her arms. We sat on the bathroom floor, both crying on each other's shoulders. I wasn't sure why she was crying but I really didn't care. She was comforting me, no questions asked. I missed her arms around me. The softness of her voice in my ear.

I pulled away and grabbed some toilet paper, dabbing my eyes before blowing my nose. Her hand moved the hair hanging in my face and placed it behind my ear.

"You're so beautiful even when you cry," she said. "I can remember when you were little, and I held you in my arms. Oh, how I've missed your hugs." Her eyes squinting, lit with an inner glow. "I recall that one time you fell and skinned your knee. Do you remember that?"

I nodded. "I fell off my bike in the driveway."

"Yes, after you were done crying, you got back on that bike and you tried again, pedaling down the sidewalk. No more tears, just a big happy smile on your face. You were so excited when you pedaled back to me. You crossed the street and rode over to Kat's house."

Amused, I nodded again, a smile spreading across my face. "Yeah, and Kat was so happy for me she grabbed her bike, and we rode up and down the street for hours." Looking at my mom, I had forgotten just how beautiful she was, especially when she smiled. It warmed my heart that she had remembered that moment.

She smoothed her hand over my hair, then caressed my cheek. "I think I'm getting too old for this," she laughed. "Hard to sit on my knees for a long time." Laughing once more before lifting herself up off the floor.

"Remind me not to get old," I said, giggling along with her. I stood, making my way to the sink. She came and stood beside me. We looked so much alike; it was unreal. "I think I'm okay now, you don't have to stay," I whispered. My eyes moved, watching her reflection in the mirror.

"Only if you're sure because I can stay if you want me to."

I did want her to stay. "No, it's okay, I'm pretty tired. I just want to sleep now."

She forced a smile and turned to face me. "Mia, I...," she reached over and kissed my cheek. "I love you no matter what, just know that okay, sweetie? I know we've had our differences, but I'm here if you want to talk. You can tell me anything."

I wanted to say I love you too, but my throat tightened. Her words sounded sincere, but I wasn't ready to confide in her. Heck, I hadn't confided in anyone about what happened. "You can't help me," I finally whispered.

Her face fell. "I'm sorry you feel that way. Let me know if you change your mind."

I held back the tears threatening to pour out of me, not wanting her to leave but not wanting her to stay either. There was a *click* when she closed the bedroom door. I looked down at the crumpled paper in my hand. I had waited so long to feel her touch again and hear her heartfelt words. Why didn't I just show her the paper? I knew why. I didn't want to disappoint her. After all, Ethan was her favorite.

Forty-Seven
Judith

After I had left Mia's room, I went downstairs to my briefcase. I dug out the paper I had hidden in the side pocket. The paper I had found in Ethan's bedroom weeks ago. My eyes moved across the words. They were the same words on the paper Mia had in the bathroom.

A wave of dizziness swept over me. Ethan had written that note to Mia. Ethan had done something to Mia. Reaching back inside the pocket, I pulled out the photos I had also found that day. I skimmed through them one by one.

"Oh, my dear God," I murmured. My body froze in mid-motion. Bile burned in the back of my throat. I ran from the office to the bathroom in the hall. Standing over the sink, I splashed water on my face. An uncontrollable shudder swept through my entire body. I grabbed the counter, holding myself up.

Lifting the photographs, I scanned the pictures again. I had to bring the photo closer to my face because I wasn't sure if I had seen what I thought I'd seen. There was a small birthmark on the left side of the girl's ribcage. The same birthmark Mia had. My body stiffened. "Oh my God."

I swallowed, holding back the cry threatening to escape. I should march back upstairs and show these to her. Then she would have to tell me what happened. What my son did to my daughter. What her brother did to his sister. She had mentioned in the journal that something happened in the Bahamas with Ethan, but never said what it was.

Another wave of sickness spread through me, making my legs weak. I moved toward the toilet, resting my back against the wall before slinking to the floor. I wasn't sure I could make it back upstairs.

~

My eyes jolted open when I heard a knock on the door. Coolness pressed against my cheek. I noticed the long narrow view to the door in front of me. I was lying on the floor in the downstairs bathroom.

"Jud, are you in there?" Scott asked, opening the door, and sticking his head inside. "Oh, my God!" He threw the door open and rushed over to me. "Jud, hon, are you all right? Are you hurt? Sick? Should I call an ambulance?"

"No, no. I'm fine," I replied. Scott helped as I pushed myself up to a sitting position and sat back against the wall.

He placed a hand on my forehead. "Are you sure you're feeling, okay?"

"Yes, hon, I'm better now. Just felt a little sick last night when I came downstairs. No need to worry."

"That is something I will always do," he replied, brushing his knuckles across my cheek.

His eyes moved to the floor where the pictures lay scattered around me.

"What are these?" he asked.

Before I could stop him, his hand gathered a few of the photos from the floor. Skimming through each picture one by one, his eyes widened. "Are these?" His eyes were rapidly blinking. "Judith, what are these? Where did you get them?"

There was disgust in his voice. The same disgust I felt when I looked at the photos of the naked girls. I swallowed, wanting nothing more than to lie to him. To tell him they were from a patient of mine, but I didn't want to keep Ethan's secret any longer. I couldn't keep it. The secret was eating me up inside. The truth was in front of him. It was time to release the pain I had held for weeks.

"I found them in Ethan's room. Inside his nightstand."

His eyes flashed to mine, waiting for me to tell him I was just kidding. *Ha, Ha.* His Adam's apple bobbed as he swallowed. Was he going to get sick?

"Ethan took these?"

I nodded. The temperature in my body was rising, making my forehead perspire. He picked up a few more photos off the floor and scanned them. I held my breath waiting for him to say something. Waiting for him to see what I saw last night. He brought the picture closer to his face, his eyes examining the photo. Then he looked at me, his mouth wide open.

"Jud, is this…" He glanced back down at the picture in his hand before holding it out in front of my face. He tapped the photo in the same spot of the birthmark. "Is this Mia? Tell me this isn't our daughter. That he…" His voice trailed off.

Shaking my head, wanting to remove the image from my mind. "I'm sorry."

"Sorry? Why are you sorry?" His eyes narrowed in on mine. "Is this Mia?" he asked again. "Ethan took pictures of our daughter. Did he? Jud, please tell me he didn't do what I think he did."

"I'm so sorry," I said, again in a low whisper.

He glanced back down at the photo, then back up at me. "Did you know about this?" His voice accusatory.

"No!" I shrieked. "Not exactly." My eyes shifted away.

"What do you mean, not exactly? What aren't you telling me?"

I started from the beginning, telling him what happened that day with Ethan in his room and what I did after he had left the house. "I hadn't noticed until last night that Mia was one of the girls in the photos."

"But you knew about these other girls and didn't say anything to me? You kept these from me?" He glared at me. "I thought we didn't keep secrets, Jud."

I had seen him like this only a handful of times. Scott wasn't a man that was easily angered. He was always so calm and cheerful. But he had a right to be upset. I had kept this from him.

"We don't, and it wasn't my intention not to tell you. I sort of forgot."

"Forgot? You came across these inappropriate pictures, and you forgot to mention it?"

"I wanted to tell you but there was so much going on. Mia was still in the hospital and Ethan went off to college. I needed time to think. I'm sorry. I know it was wrong." Tears were leaking from my eyes. "I just couldn't bring myself to tell you yet. I had put them in my briefcase. Out of sight, out of mind. I wasn't thinking straight. I'm sorry. I'm so, so sorry," I pleaded, tears streaming down my face. My heart was aching with sadness.

He blew out a breath, skimming the photos once again before tossing them back onto my lap. "We're going upstairs and we're going to talk to Mia right now. This could be why she..." He slid over to the wall behind him and placed his head in his hands.

It wasn't often that I had seen Scott cry. "Scott..." I hesitated, moving to sit beside him. "What should we do about Ethan?"

His head shot up. "Ethan? At this fucking moment, I don't give a shit about Ethan! My concern is talking to Mia and finding out what happened. That's it, nothing else. We will deal with him later!"

Forty-Eight
<u>Mia</u>

When I walked down the stairs the following morning, voices sounded from down the hall. Their bedroom door had been closed and I assumed they were still sleeping. It wasn't even seven in the morning yet. Part of me wanted to eavesdrop on their conversation but didn't want to hear what they had to say about me. Because in all honesty, who else could they be talking about?

I stepped off the last wooden step and made my way into the kitchen, heading straight to the coffee pot. While the coffee brewed, I gathered a couple frying pans and placed them on the stove. My dad and I always made breakfast together on the weekends. Opening the fridge, I took out the eggs, bacon, milk and OJ, and placed them on the counter.

"Hey, you're up early."

I peered around the refrigerator door. My dad stood in the doorway. "I could say the same about you. You want me to help with breakfast?" I asked.

"Yes, of course," he replied, walking toward the sink.

He seemed a little off this morning, not his usual cheerful self, and I wondered what they were talking about minutes ago. Though, I probably already knew.

"I smell coffee." My mom walked into the kitchen, looking haggard. Had she even slept last night after she left my room? What the hell was going on with my parents?

"Mia," my dad said. "Your mom and I need to…," he turned and looked at my mom. "We need to talk to you about something."

Shutting the refrigerator door, I looked at the both of them. Were they cornering me? To get me to talk about what happened? I didn't like the feeling that came over me. If I didn't know any better, they were teaming up against me. I knew, but was hoping they would just let what had happened go, praying they would ignore it. I get it, I do. They were my parents' wanting answers, which meant they cared but it wouldn't change what had happened to me. What *he* did to me.

"Do you want to do this now or after we eat?" I asked.

"We can talk about it after breakfast," my mom chimed in, looking at my dad for clarification.

~

The three of us sat on the sofa in the family room. My stomach was queasy with anticipation. Maybe this was a bad idea. Maybe we should have done this before we ate. It was a delicate topic we were about to unfold. Or maybe we shouldn't discuss this at all. It wasn't going to be what they wanted to hear.

"Mia," my mom said. "Before we show you something, we want to know if you want to talk to us about why you felt suicide was a way out. Did something happen that you couldn't live with or thought you couldn't come to us about?"

"We care about you, Mia. We want to help you with whatever it is you're battling," my dad said.

Sitting back into the overstuffed loveseat, while my parents sat on the sofa in front of me, vigorously rubbing my hands as they talked. I wanted to jump off the chair, run to my bedroom, and lock the door. Mentally, I wasn't sure I could tell them what had happened that led me to want to die. Then again, I didn't want to keep it locked inside me anymore. It was destroying me from the inside out. I had troubles eating, sleeping, and felt mentally unstable.

"I uh, found these and well, I want you to take a look at them," mom said, holding out her hand filled with photos.

Hesitantly, I grabbed them, but didn't look at them. My eyes were still observing their movements, waiting for more. Why would they be handing me a stack of pictures? Then a memory flashed in my head. Oh, my God! Were these? In an instant I wanted to flee from the room and hide.

"Mia, please look at them," dad whispered.

Shifting my eyes from the photos then to my parents and back to the photos in my hand. They were pictures of other girls, not of me. How many girls did he…? How long had he been doing this? My stomach dropped, feeling sick again like last night. I looked at the next picture, then the next until I was staring down at the photo of me. Oh God! They know. Lifting my eyes, I saw the look on my parent's faces. It wasn't a look of disappointment but of concern. My mouth opened, but no words came out. No, no, no. I couldn't do this. I couldn't turn their world upside down and ruin this family, but wasn't our family already ruined by *him*?

"Mia did Ethan hurt you?" mom asked. Tears leaked from my eyes. She stood and hurried to my side. "Oh, baby, I'm so sorry." She enveloped me into her arms. "You need to tell us what he did to you. We need to know so we can help you."

"We need to make sure he never does this to anyone ever again," dad said.

I looked from mom to dad and then down at my lap where the photos still lay. *My brother not only did this to me but to other girls too,* my head repeated. No matter how damaged I was inside. I needed to tell them everything. I can't let him hurt anyone else.

"It started on our trip to the Bahamas. I woke up on the second night with Ethan standing at the foot of my bed. I thought he was sleepwalking or something. So, I climbed out of bed and stood in front of him. He then grabbed my arms and pressed his lips against mine." I began to cry. "I wanted to tell you but didn't think you'd believe me. He's your favorite," I said looking at my mom. "You always believe everything he says."

"I...I didn't realize you thought that. I've always loved you just the same," mom replied.

"What happened after that?" dad asked.

"Besides some uncomfortable stares the rest of the trip, he didn't do anything until," I choked back a cry.

"Until what?" mom whispered. She was now crying too.

"When I was out with Trevor, I swore I had seen Ethan hanging around, hiding in the background, watching me. I don't know if he was waiting to see if I'd say something to Trevor about what he'd done, but then he would disappear. I didn't see him again until the weekends when he came home. Then..." I swallowed the bile rising in the back of my throat. "He would leave messages in my room when I was sleeping. Saying he was watching me." My throat constricted and I began to hyperventilate.

"Breathe," mom said beside me. She embraced me in her arms, rocking me like she did when I was a child.

After several breaths, my stomach calmed down. The anxiety was slowly shrinking away. "Then, one day when no one was home, he ran after me through the house and..." *Tears bled from my eyes.* "He chased me upstairs. I tried to get into my room and lock the door, but he...he grabbed me from behind and dragged me to his bedroom and..." I clenched my stomach and ran out of the room to the bathroom in the hall. My breakfast now filled the toilet.

"Shh," my mom said beside me as she held my hair out of my face and rubbed my back. "Did he rape you?" she whispered.

I turned to face her. I didn't need to say anything, the evidence was written all over my face. She began to cry in a way I had never seen her do. But mostly what warmed my heart; she was crying for me.

Forty-Nine

Judith

After finally getting Mia to lie down in bed and fall asleep, I stepped out into the hall. My entire body shook with grief and fear. I was filled with disgust at what my son did to my daughter. His own sister…I hurried down the hall to my room and closed the door. Tears poured from my eyes.

My daughter was willing to take her own life over what *he* had done to her. Ethan had been close to his sister his whole life, but to hurt her physically and emotionally. Where had I gone wrong with him? I needed to go downstairs and talk to Scott. We needed to do something about our son.

Scott was still sitting on the sofa when I came back downstairs. My eyes were red and puffy.

"How's she doing?"

"I finally got her to fall asleep, but she's going to need a therapist. There may be things she can't talk to us about and will need someone to talk to," I replied, sitting next to him.

He reached for my hand and squeezed it. "We're going to the police," he said. "I want Ethan arrested for what he did to Mia and to those other girls."

I nodded. "Let's call Dave from across the street and talk to him first. Maybe he can tell us the best way to handle this."

"Yeah, okay, let's call him." Scott slipped his cell from his jeans and opened his contacts. "Hey, Dave, it's Scott from across the street. Are you home by any chance?"

My ears perked up to the muffled sound of his voice through the receiver.

"Yeah, it's best you come to our place. I'll tell you everything once you get here." He ended the call. "He'll be right over."

It had only been a couple of minutes before there was a knock on the front door. Scott stood and opened the door.

"Hey, what's so urgent you couldn't tell me on the phone?" Dave asked, stepping inside.

"Let's talk in here," Scott said, motioning to the chair in the family room.

I wasn't sure I could hold it together, so I let Scott do all the talking.

"So, that night I came running over here and found you and Mia in the bathroom, she tried to end her life because of what Ethan did?" Dave asked.

"Yes, but Mia couldn't tell us in detail what had happened to her. She couldn't get the words out. Judith did ask her if she had been raped by her brother and she said yes," Scott replied, looking from me to Dave.

"I want my son arrested for what he did," I said. "Not only for what he did to Mia but also the other girls."

Dave sat in the chair across from us going through the photos. "Do you know any of these girls? Did Mia?" Dave asked.

We both shook our heads.

"No, she didn't say anything. It was too traumatic for her to tell us what happened."

Dave nodded. "The question is, do you want us to go to his school and arrest him or do you want to call him home and we can do it here? I'll call my buddy at work and have him meet us here."

Scott and I looked at one another. "I'll call him and ask for him to come home. I'm surprised he isn't home this weekend, being that Monday is a holiday," I said.

We all turned when the front door opened, and Ethan walked in. He stopped in the doorway and scanned the room, resting his eyes on Dave. Or should I say what was in his hands.

"Hey son, why don't you come in and have a seat," Scott said.

"Nah, I have things to do," Ethan replied.

Dave stood and walked to Ethan. "Son, I think you should take a seat."

"I'm not your son and like I said, I have things to do!" Ethan growled.

Dave grabbed Ethan's arm just as he went to walk away. "You're not going anywhere. Sit down!" Dave demanded.

Ethan tried to yank his arm from Dave's grip but didn't succeed. Dave led him to the chair and pushed him down. He stood in front of him so he couldn't flee. He removed his cell from his front pocket and dialed a number. Seconds later, he pushed the phone back into the pocket of his jeans.

"What is this all about?" Ethan asked.

"I think you know," Dave replied, handing him the pictures. "You're under arrest for raping the girls in the photos and…"

"And for raping Mia!" I said, with a guttural roar. "You are not welcome in this house. I want a restraining order against him. He is never to come near Mia or us again." Heat burned my cheeks with each word. "You are not my son!" I screamed. Scott placed a hand on my arm, but I yanked it away. Jumping to my feet, I hurried out of the room. It made me sick to be near him. He was no longer my son. I wanted him in jail for the rest of his life.

When I stepped inside the hall, I spotted Mia at the top of the landing staring down at me. Racing up the stairs, I wrapped an arm around her, escorting her back to her bedroom.

"Mom," Mia whispered. "Is that Ethan I hear?"

Once inside her room, I closed the door and locked it. "Yes, sweetie. He's downstairs with your dad and Dave from across the street."

"Are they arresting him?"

"Yes. I'm also getting a restraining order against him. He will never hurt you again. Or anyone else for that matter." I folded her into my arms as we both wept. "I'm so sorry I didn't protect you."

Mia pulled away and looked me in the eyes. "You didn't know. How could you protect me from something you didn't know was happening?"

Of course she was right, but it still didn't make me feel any better. "I promise you, nothing bad will ever happen to you again."

"You can't know that," Mia stated. "I know you have good intentions, but you can't protect me from everything bad that will happen in my life, Mom."

My fingers brushed the strains of hair away from her face and tucked them behind her ear. "I know, I should've…"

"What? You should've known." Mia muttered. "How could you? He fooled us all. Me, Dad, and you."

"I'm your mother, I still…"

"No, you couldn't have known." Mia slumped down on the edge of her bed. "I know I should have come and talked to you about what he did. I just… I just thought you wouldn't believe me."

I knelt in front of her, lifting her chin so we were eye to eye. "Don't you ever for one second think I wouldn't believe you. What he did to you, I…I will never forgive him for that." There was a tightness in my chest, making it hard to breathe. I stood and sat beside her, wanting nothing more than for this day to be over.

I lifted her arm and caressed the thick scar on her arm. "He hurt you to the point you felt suicide was a way out. I can never forgive him for that. He will never be a part of this family again."

Mia leaned into me, and I wrapped an arm around her. "Mom?"

"Yes, sweetie."

"I'm sorry for being so mean to you all these years. I…I love you. I hope you can forgive me."

"Oh, Mia. Yes, of course, I forgive you. Can you forgive me for working all the time and not being the mother, you needed? I promise to be better," I replied, squeezing her into me.

"Mom, I think we are both to blame."

"Yeah, maybe you're right," I said, and kissed her head. "But I will do better by you and for you."

Fifty

Mia

There was a soft knock on the door. I glanced at my mom who sat next to me, her complexion pale. The tap came again, and I stood.

"It's me, Dad, can you open the door please?"

Turning the lock, I opened the door. My dad stood in front of me, his expression soft. He leaned in and wrapped me in his arms. Seconds later, he pulled away, looking into my eyes.

"I'm so sorry, baby girl."

"Don't. I told Mom the same thing. It's not your fault, so please stop apologizing for what *he* did." They were making it hard to be strong when they were the ones that needed to be strong for me.

Dad nodded. "Okay, I'll try. I just…"

My mom stood beside me now. "Is *he* still here?"

"No, Dave and Officer Wallace came to the house and took him to the station. He's been arrested and charged with multiple counts of rape, abuse, and underage pornography."

My posture slumped with relief. I was safe now and for the first time since the assault, I released everything I held inside me and cried. He couldn't hurt me any longer. Stepping back, my knees touched the side of the bed, and I plopped down, placing my face in my hands. My body shook as I wept. I felt both of my parents next to me. They wrapped their arms around me and held me tight.

"It's going to be all right," mom said. "We're here for you and we will do whatever we have to, to help you and keep you safe."

"We love you so much Mia," dad said.

"I love you too," I whispered.

~

A couple of hours later, I was sitting cross-legged on the floor in Kat's bedroom. I needed to get out of the house for a while. She hadn't asked me what was wrong, and I hadn't said anything since I arrived less than an hour ago. Was she putting all the pieces together like she always did? Detective Kat to the rescue. Even if she hadn't put the pieces together, she would eventually.

"So, do you want to tell me what happened?" she asked. "Why my dad had to go over to your house. Why they took Ethan away in a police car?"

Well, that didn't take long. I couldn't lie to her; she'd find out eventually and it would tear us apart again. She was my friend. My best friend! I shrugged my shoulders at the question, but when I lifted my eyes to look at her, she was looking down at the floor. She must have felt me watching her because she lifted her head. We did that for another few minutes before she spoke, again.

"I know we just started being friends again, but I want you to know that I'm here for you. No matter what," she emphasized, grabbing my hand, and squeezing it. "You can tell me anything. I swear to you, I won't breathe a word to anyone." She lifted her other hand and made an X sign over her heart just like we used to do when we were kids.

As if struck from behind without the force of someone hitting me, the words flew out of my mouth. Words I never wanted to say to anyone again. Words I wanted to keep hidden. Words I had spoken this morning to my parents. The words tasted bitter, almost like biting into a piece of rotten fruit. "I was raped." I rubbed my free hand against the skin of my arm hoping to generate heat. Just saying those three words made the room feel like death had breezed in.

Kat gasped and her hand flew to her mouth. "R…raped?" The single word slipped from her lips as if tainted by a poisonous snake. Her forehead wrinkled with concern, then her eyes dropped to the floor.

Why couldn't she look at me? Was she repulsed by the sight of me now? Like I was some disgusting, awful, dead animal lying on the road after being hit by a car? Or was this her way of processing what I'd said? Even though I haven't said anything else.

A second later, she flung herself toward me, almost knocking me over. Her arms wrapped around me, squeezing me tight. "I'm so sorry," she said. "Why didn't you... I mean you could have talked to me."

She pulled away; her face streaked with tears. She slid her hands down my arms, resting near the scars on my wrists. Flipping my hands over, she smoothed her thumb across each scar. Her eyes shifted back up. Tears were still streaming down her face. Kat wasn't someone who cried easily, but I also haven't been around her in a long time. People change. I've changed.

"When did this happen? Is that why you..." She couldn't finish the sentence. She didn't need to finish the sentence.

"July and yes."

She threw her arms around me again, clutching me tighter this time.

"Kat, I can't breathe," I croaked in a whisper.

She let out a low chuckle before letting her arms loosen from around me. "Sorry."

How many times do I have to hear the word sorry. We seemed to stare at one another which was better than talking. I didn't want to tell her who. She already knew when it had happened, well, not the precise day. She really didn't need to know any of that. I didn't want to talk about *it* period, but the can of worms were open and spilling out. Now… now I had to say something that would keep her from asking more questions.

"Mia, I'm so sorry," she whispered. "I know you said you don't want to tell me but I'm here for you. Whenever you're ready to talk to someone."

I nodded, relief rolling over me.

Then as if a switch had flicked on in her head. "Wait," she said, her eyes narrowing in on mine. "Is that why Ethan was arrested? Did he…"

My stomach dropped. Words weren't needed when my face gave her the answer.

"Oh my God, Mia, Ethan? My dad will make sure he rots in jail," she spat. "He will not see the light of day again."

"There's more."

"More?"

"There were other girls he did this too, not just me."

"What?" she sucked in a breath.

My head jerked toward the bedroom door. There was a scuffing sound on the other side of the door. Kat seemed comatose before jumping to her feet and hurrying to the door. Eva came strolling in, placing her snout against my face.

I smiled. "Hey, girl," I said, stroking a hand through her long, soft blonde fur.

She let out a snort and I laughed.

"Even she knows you need someone to lean on," Kat said.

I kissed Eva on the side of her face before she sat down beside me. Placing an arm over her back, she leaned into me, nearly knocking me over with her weight. I began to laugh harder as I fell to the floor. Eva pounced on me like I were a toy.

"Eva!" Kat shouted. "Get off her."

Eva turned toward Kat but didn't move. I ruffled her fur and she barked playfully.

"It's fine, I love playing with her."

"I think she feels the same way," Kat replied, with a laugh.

I laid there on the bedroom floor playing with Eva, when a burst of sharp, piercing pain shot through my abdomen. Clutching my stomach, I rolled over onto my side.

"Mia, are you all right?"

"No, I don't think so," I said through gritted teeth. I screamed when another surge of pain blasted through me.

"Oh my God, Mia!"

I peered up at my friend with a clenched jaw, holding my midsection tightly.

Kat moved from a sitting position to her knees beside me and placed a hand on my arm. "What do you want me to do? Should I call for an ambulance?"

I shook my head. I didn't want to go to the hospital. Her eyes shifted from my face to the floor behind me where I was sitting.

"Umm, Mia. I think there's something wrong."

Of course, there was something wrong. I was lying on my side, on her bedroom floor in agony. Then I felt a warm sensation between my legs.

Fifty-One
Judith

With everything that had happened this morning, Scott and I had decided to go for a drive. We both wanted to get out of the house and left after Mia had gone over to her friend Kat's house.

Staring out the passenger window, I replayed the recent parts of my life that had led me to this very moment. I used my work as a crutch, making it first before Mia, before my family. By the time I got home, my daughter was locked away in her room. Even at dinnertime she sat quietly on one side of the dining room table, picking at her food. We asked about school, or I should say, Scott did. I was usually still stuck in my head with patients I had seen that day. I never made time to prioritize my family life with my work life. As part of my work ethic, it was a means to escape the things that frightened me the most. A way to escape reality with the issues I had at home with my daughter. The abuse my father put upon me and my mother. When I turned eighteen, I left that part of my life behind. I never went back to my childhood home to visit my parents, who are now both deceased.

The vehicle slowed, snapping me from my thoughts. I hadn't seen a sign telling me where we were when he turned left onto a gravel road.

"I haven't been here in ages," Scott said.

I glanced over at him, listening as he talked, yet my mind was still on Mia. I couldn't stop thinking about her. She needed me and I was out driving around with Scott instead of staying with her.

"My father used to bring the whole family here when we were little. Isn't it beautiful?"

I turned away from him and looked out the windshield. A sense of calm filled my chest. Something I hadn't felt in a while. I couldn't wait to see a part of his childhood. After twenty some years together, I wondered why he hadn't brought me here before?

The vehicle settled to a stop as he put the car in park. Scott opened the driver's side door and climbed out, making his way to my side. He was such a gentleman, always had been. The moment he opened the passenger door, I inhaled the earthy smell of pine needles and wildflowers. The scent was enticing, and I felt entranced like I was floating in a field of sweetness.

He interlaced his fingers with mine and guided us down a trail. The dotting path was layered with slate pieces, pebbles, and pine needles. Scott skidded to a stop. I moved from behind him and stood at his side.

"It's beautiful," I whispered. The view was stunning. I never thought there was a place like this in Ohio, but I also haven't traveled much in my life.

I gazed out over the cliff in front of us. I wasn't sure how far the drop was to the bottom. There was the sound of rushing water from a creek or river in the distance. Feeling at peace for the first time in a long time, I stood there soaking in the radiant blue sky. The bright sun beamed down on us, filling me with warmth on this September day. Overhead, birds were flying in a continuous circle before resting on the nearby tree branches. To my left was a rabbit. Its nose was sniffing the air before it hopped behind the tree, now out of site.

"My dad would bring us here and we would have a picnic. Then when my mom died," he swallowed. "I haven't come back here since."

There was a sadness in his voice when he spoke of his mother. I had never had the pleasure of meeting her because she had passed away when Scott was twelve from breast cancer. I squeezed his hand before folding into him. He wrapped an arm around me, kissing the top of my head.

"I'll be right back," he said, leaving me standing there, missing his presence.

Minutes later, he came walking back down the path holding a large blanket, one I hadn't known was in the car. He unfolded it and placed it on the ground. Reaching a hand out, he led me to the center of the blanket. We sat facing the stunning view; his arm wrapped around me.

There were no words to express what my eyes were witnessing, but the scenery took my breath away. How could something so beautiful even exist? I soaked in every bit of the landscape. Never wanted to leave this very spot. Feeling mesmerized by the blue skies and the sounds of nature.

"Judith?"

"Yeah," I mumbled, sinking into him.

"We need to talk about what happened with Mia."

My heart seemed to stop momentarily. I didn't want to think about this morning. What our family had been through this past month. I fought hard to push it out of my head during the drive and now he wanted me to dig up the memories. He wanted to talk about it when I just wanted to forget. Not that I could ever forget.

"What do you think we should do about Ethan?"

I tilted my face toward him, squinting. "As far as I'm concerned, he's no longer my son, Scott. He hurt Mia, our daughter, and let's not forget the other girls. Girls we don't even know."

He nodded. "I'm glad we're on the same page. I want to find the other girls. I want him to pay for hurting them."

Fifty-Two
Mia

There was a circle of blood the size of a cantaloupe on the floor behind me. I placed a hand between my legs and when I pulled it away, blood coated my fingers.

Blood.

There was so much blood. I glanced over at Kat who quickly stood and sprinted from the room, returning a few seconds later with some towels.

"Here put this under you."

"I'm sorry. I'm so sorry," I sobbed, then another jolt of pain ripped through my abdomen.

"Mia, I think…I think you're having a miscarriage."

Miscarriage? How can I be having a…? The thought froze in my mind, recalling the last time I had sex. "No, no, no, this can't be happening."

"Here let's go into the bathroom and get you into the shower."

Kat helped me to my feet, led me to the bathroom and into the shower. I unbuttoned my pants, and she helped me remove my jeans, but I left on my panties. I already felt embarrassed about bleeding all over her bedroom floor, I didn't need to be sitting in her bathtub naked.

Kat gasped when she looked at me. "Mia, you're so… thin."

I peered down at my body even though I knew what I looked like, then back up at her.

She turned on the water. I sat on the floor of the tub; warm water washing the blood down the drain. The cramping continued, some more severe than others.

"You have to go to the hospital," Kat demanded. "There could be something else wrong."

My body trembled but I didn't feel cold. Was my body going into shock? I remember in sex education class when the teacher talked about pregnancies and what could happen to a woman who was having a miscarriage.

"Have you been having any kind of pain before today?" Kat asked.

"Actually, yes. A few different times."

"What kind of pain? It says online that you can experience dull back pain, severe belly pain, fever, weight loss, and weakness. These are all symptoms of a miscarriage, Mia."

My mind scanned back over the past few weeks, but it was only the last couple of days that I recalled not feeling well. Then it hit me, when I was in the hospital, I had been throwing up a lot, which were signs of morning sickness.

"Do you think…?" she paused.

"What Kat?"

"When was the last time you had unprotected sex?"

I didn't have to think too hard about the question because Trevor and I hadn't had sex since this past summer which meant...

"Mia, I can tell by your face that something is wrong. You know you can talk to me. You can trust me."

"I know I can, it's just..."

"What?" Kat sat down on the floor, her back against the wall. "I swear to you I won't say a word to anyone. Not my dad or Jim."

I bowed my head, knowing I could trust her. I needed to start trusting someone with what had happened to me.

~

As the minutes ticked by, the pain subsided, and the bleeding slowed. We were both sure that I had had a miscarriage. Though, I hadn't known I was pregnant. This explained everything I had been feeling in the last month.

Relief fell over me. I wouldn't have wanted to keep the baby anyway. I was too young, and it wasn't Trevor's. *It wasn't Trevor's,* my mind repeated.

"I still think you need to go to the hospital," Kat stressed.

I started to shake my head when I doubled over in pain, again. A scream erupted from deep inside me. I wrapped my arms around my midsection, hoping that it would ease the pain, but it didn't.

"That's it, I'm calling for help," Kat shouted, jumping to her feet and running out of the room.

As much as I wanted to stop her, I couldn't. The pain was too intense. I'm not sure how much time had passed when I heard a male voice.

"Ma'am, can you hear me?" a man asked.

My head felt heavy as I tried to lift it. My eyes fluttered open then closed. Feeling dizzy and drained like I hadn't slept in days. Just how much blood had I lost?

I couldn't pinpoint where the voices were coming from, but I was sure he was beside me. A hand lifted my head. I blinked heavily and saw the man's face in front of me. He was dressed in a dark blue jacket with a logo of a medical symbol and the letters EMS under it.

"Let's get her out of the bathtub and onto the stretcher," the male EMT said.

"Do you know how long your friend has been like this?" a different voice asked. A female voice I hadn't known was in the room with us. Was she talking to me? I wasn't sure and tried to speak. The muscles in my jaw tightened. I grinded my teeth and clutched my midsection as another sharp pain surfaced.

"Maybe an hour, I think. I don't know. I can't be certain," Kat said. "I wasn't watching the clock. I should've been watching the clock."

There was panic in her voice. My friend was scared for me. God, what did I do? I shouldn't have come over here. My best friend had just lost her mom and now I was in a fetal position in her shower bleeding to death just like I was over a month ago when my mom found me. At that second, I thought about my mom and how she must have felt when she discovered me in the tub. Did she panic like Kat was doing at this moment? The doctor did tell me that my mom was the one who found me. Who had saved me.

"It's fine. Don't blame yourself. We're here now, and we will get your friend the help she needs," the female EMT replied, calming Kat with her soothing words.

"She started having abdominal pain and then the blood…So, I brought her in here. She didn't want me to call for help, but I just had to. She was screaming from all the pain. I couldn't let her…", Kat said before choking back a sob.

"You did the right thing," the male EMT said. "She'll be fine now, but we need to get her to the hospital. She's weak and has lost a lot of blood."

They lifted and positioned me on the stretcher. I felt exposed until a sheet was placed over my body, covering my nakedness.

"Can I go with her?" Kat asked.

"Yes, but you'll need to get ahold of her parents. They'll need to know what is happening and to meet us at the hospital," the male EMT replied.

My parents. Where were my parents? They had to have seen the ambulance pull up to Kat's house. They'd be outside watching. They'd see me being wheeled out of the house. But once we were outside, the streets were empty. I didn't see anyone standing on the sidewalk. My parents were nowhere in sight.

~

Lights glimmered all around me as I opened my eyes. Voices low and high shouted out commands. Their words were getting twisted in the fog of my brain. I was at the hospital but where was Kat?

Turning my head, I looked to the left and then to the right. I didn't see her anywhere, which meant she'd have to be in the waiting room. Were my parents there too? Had she been able to get in touch with them?

"She's hemorrhaging. We need to get her in the OR stat," someone demanded.

Were they talking to me or about me? A plastic mask was being placed over my nose and mouth. Then there was movement as they wheeled me out of the room and down a narrow hall. A bright light hung down from the ceiling and the bed came to a stop. A face wearing a light blue mask appeared in front of my eyes.

"Count to ten," she said to me.

One, two, three, and then everything went black…

Fifty-Three
Judith

Thunder rumbled in the distance. A gust of wind rattled the tall trees around us. I felt it against my face, drying my lips. The wind whipped my hair from the clip I had placed on the back of my head. How much time had passed while we sat looking out over the cliff?

I tilted my head back and looked up. The sky had changed from a bright blue to a heavy gray. The trees swayed and moaned from side-to-side. Then, a drop of rain splattered into my eye, making me blink. In the amount of time it took to breathe in a lung full of air; the heavens above opened their flood gates and rain poured from the sky.

Scott didn't waste a second as he sprung to his feet, holding out a hand which I clutched and scurried to my feet. I slipped, my knee nearly hitting the ground. He snatched the blanket and covered our heads with it. I wasn't sure what came over us as we began to laugh under the thick, wool blanket. There was nothing funny about being stuck in the pouring rain, but it did feel good to laugh.

We rushed up the trail. The rainwater was turning the dry dirt to mud. Once up the hill, I spotted our car in the distance. Scott's grip tightened. He squeezed my hand, pulling me behind him. He held the door open for me and I slipped into the passenger seat. Seconds later, he jumped in behind the wheel beside me, the blanket still covering his head.

"Wow! That seemed to come out of nowhere," I laughed.

"You're telling me. Maybe that's a sign?"

I gazed into his eyes. I wasn't someone that believed in magic or things happening for a reason. It was just the way life was. Wasn't it? Now I seemed to be questioning myself. "A sign?"

"That something terrible has happened or is about to. I think we need to get home."

My eyes hadn't moved. I was still looking at Scott. Still searching his face for answers. Why would he say something like that? Hadn't something terrible already happened? *Mia,* my mind whispered. *Has something happened to her besides what we just found out?*

"Sorry, I know you don't believe in all that hocus pocus." He squeezed my hand that was laying on my leg. "Everything is going to be all right. I promise you. We're her parents and we'll be there for her no matter what."

Parents, my mind repeated. I couldn't ever recall my parents being there for me. My father did the yelling as my mother, the coward, hid in the kitchen or in another room. She was afraid of him, but so was I.

I nodded in response. "Yes, of course we will be there for her." I whispered and turned back toward the passenger window, thinking of nothing but Mia.

Fifty-Four

Mia

Wooziness swept over me when, I opened my eyes, so I closed them, waiting for the feeling to vanish. A flood of images flashed through my mind, recalling what had happened earlier that had led me to be in the hospital.

"Mia."

My eyes sprung open, searching through the dimly lit room. Kat's silhouette appeared beside the bed.

"Mia," she whispered again. A smile played on her lips. "I'm so glad you're okay. God, I was so worried about you." She wrapped her arms around her chest, hugging herself.

I waited but she didn't say anything more. "How long have I been out?"

She turned and scanned the wall. I followed her gaze. A clock was positioned near the TV mounted on the wall.

"A few hours. You were in surgery for a while and then they brought you in here."

Surgery? "They had to do surgery on me. I don't remember," I replied, searching my mind for anything since being at Kat's house and all that blood gushing out of me. "What about my parents? Did you get a hold of them? Are they mad?"

She shook her head. "No, I couldn't get ahold of them. But why would they be mad at you? I think they would be more concerned Mia, not mad."

Her eyes avoided mine. Was she hiding something from me? Her focus was on the linoleum floor.

"Kat, what's going on?" Before she could answer, we both turned our heads toward the door. A woman walked into the room.

"Oh, good, you're awake," said a woman, wearing blue and white scrubs. Her hair was pulled back into a bun on the top of her head. She walked over and checked the monitors beside me and made some adjustments. "How are you feeling? Do you have any pain?"

"I'm good. No pain. Can you tell me what happened when I got to the hospital?" I asked.

"Sorry, I was just assigned to your room." She observed me, then looked over at Kat. "I'll go let the doctor know you're awake and he can talk to you," the nurse said and scurried out of the room.

I had the feeling something wasn't right. I turned and viewed Kat who looked paler than normal. "Are you all right? Do you know what the doctor is going to tell me?" She shook her head. "Kat?" I questioned. "If you know something, please tell me."

"There was so much blood. They said you were hemorrhaging. That's why you had to have surgery. To stop the bleeding."

Searching through my memory, I didn't recall hearing those words. "Kat, I think you should sit down before you fall over." She walked over to the chair by the window and dragged it over to the side of the bed. The air in the cushion hissed as she lowered herself onto the seat. This had to be hard on her after losing her mom. Though when I had gone to her house earlier today, I hadn't known any of this was going to happen so I couldn't blame myself.

"Did you call Trevor?" I asked.

"No, I didn't know if you wanted me too. You know, after what you told me." She seemed to get whiter the more she spoke.

"Thank you." I know I have to tell him sooner rather than later. Though in all honesty, I didn't want to tell him at all.

"It's good to see you are alert," a husky, male voice said from across the room. The short, thick-framed man with a shiny head waltzed into the room. The white coat he was wearing hung just above his knees. He stopped at the foot of the bed, his eyes scanning over the digital device he was holding. He tapped and swiped before turning his attention back to me.

"How's your pain level?"

"Um, I'm not having any right now."

"Can you give me a number from one to ten? Ten being the worst pain you've ever experienced."

"I guess, one."

"Good. That's good." He tapped a finger on the screen.

"My friend said you had to do surgery on me."

He nodded before looking up from the device and glancing from me to Kat. "Yes, you were…"

"Hemorrhaging," I stated.

"How old are you?"

"I'm seventeen."

"I see. And where are your parents? Or guardians? Do you want them present when I tell you?"

I looked toward Kat, shaking my head, then turned back to the doctor. "I'm not sure where my parents are, but you can tell me without them here."

"Well, whatever I tell you does fall under doctor/patient confidentially. So, they don't need to be present if you don't want them to be."

I didn't respond so he continued.

"You had what we call a maternal hemorrhage. The amount of damage done…" he hesitated. "Not to confuse you with medical terms. I'm afraid that you will not be able to get pregnant again. There was too much damage to your uterus, and we had to remove it."

Kat gasped beside me.

My jaw dropped as the words filtered inside my head.

I would never be able to have a baby.

Fifty-Five
Judith

Rain splattered the windshield, giving us no signs of it stopping anytime soon. Scott slowed the car down as it became impossible to see. Thankful we were the only ones out on the road, at least that I could see.

A bolt of lightning burst, illuminating the clouds in the distance. Flashes of the night I had found Mia whipped through my mind. There was a storm that night too. Praying that the feeling Scott had earlier didn't have anything to do with Mia. *Please let her be okay.*

The wipers thrashed back and forth. The rain pelted the ground in volumes. Nervousness spun in my stomach; I was afraid that we would hit the large water puddles and hydroplane off the road. There was a tightness in my chest, one that felt all too familiar. I turned my head and looked over at Scott who was gripping the steering wheel, his knuckles turning white. He didn't look at me, keeping his focus only on the road. Turning my head back, I looked out the windshield. It was as if someone had flicked a switch, causing the rain to slow to a steady *plop, plop*.

A heavy grumble sounded in the distance, then a sharp crack of lightning bolted from the sky, striking the ground somewhere in front of us.

"Breathe," Scott said.

I turned back toward him, wondering how he knew I had been holding my breath. He had been focused on the road. How did he know that I was having another one of my mini panic attacks?

I released the air from my lungs and took in another breath. The tightness subsided, making me feel calmer. Making me feel normal again. I almost laughed at the thought. *Normal.* I don't think in all my life I had ever felt like a normal person. It was my past trauma that I chose to become a psychiatrist. To help others not feel the way I do sometimes.

"I think we're past the worst of the storm," he said. "Strange how it came out of nowhere."

I nodded. Just like my life since Mia's suicide. One minute it was sunny with blue skies and the next a storm filled with destruction. Scott looked out the fogged-covered windshield. Extending my arm, I turned on the defroster. The glass cleared in seconds.

A buzzing sound came from my purse on the floor. I reached inside and pulled out my phone. Kat's name appeared on the screen.

"Hello," I answered.

"Hey, Mrs. B." Kat said.

Her tone sounded worrisome through the phone. "Kat, is everything okay?" I remembered Mia saying she was going to Kat's house before we left for the drive. "Kat, is something wrong with Mia?" I questioned.

"I…I think you, no, you definitely need to come to the hospital."

"Hospital?" Frantic now, I turned, looking at Scott, who was eyeing me with concern. "What's happened? Is Mia okay?"

"Mrs. B., just get here as soon as you can. We're at Willow Memorial Hospital."

"You're scaring me, Kat. What in God's name has happened to my Mia?"

"She's fine now, but she needs you here with her. When can you get here?"

"We'll be there as soon as we can. Maybe fifteen to twenty minutes." I looked over at Scott, indicating for him to go faster. Kat hung up and I lowered the phone from my ear.

"Jud, what's going on. What's happened to Mia?" Scott's face contorted.

I swallowed, my mouth tasting like cotton. "Kat didn't say. She just wants us to get to the hospital as soon as possible. She said Mia is fine, but wouldn't tell me what happened to her."

~

Once at the hospital, I jumped out of the car, Scott on my heels. In the lobby, my eyes scanned the room for Kat, but didn't see her. I hurried to the nurse's station.

"Hi, I'm here to see my daughter. She was brought to the hospital. Her name is Mia Barnes."

"Mrs. B.," Kat shouted.

I turned in the direction of her voice.

"You made it." Kat hurried toward us.

My eyes narrowed in on Kat's face. I studied her demeanor, looking for answers. "Mia?" My stomach dropped, feeling hard as a rock. "She didn't… Suicide? Again? Oh please, no!" My heart nearly exploded, waiting for answers.

"No!" she shrieked, appearing horror struck. "She didn't. That's not why she's here. She's fine, Mrs. B., but…" Kat hesitated.

"But what? Spit it out Kat!" my voice was rising, which took me by surprise.

"Mia was at my house earlier and she… she started bleeding—like a lot. So, I called for an ambulance, and when they brought her here…" Kat looked away, then back at me. "The doctors took her into surgery."

"Surgery?" My eyes narrowed in on Kat's face. "What the fuck happened!?" I growled under my breath. Scott touched my arm, getting my attention.

Kat took a step back, looking frightened. "Mia should be the one to tell you."

"Is there somewhere we can go and talk?" Scott asked Kat, looking around the room.

"Kat!" I barked. "Just tell me what the hell happened!"

"Jud, let's go somewhere private," Scott said, placing an arm around me, guiding me away from the situation.

"I need to know Scott. I need to know what happened to her."

"And we will, but not this way," Scott replied softly. "We don't need an audience."

We followed Kat through a set of doors, then onto an elevator, stopping on the second floor. We followed her down the hall, stopping outside room 229.

Kat hugged herself tight, staring down at the floor. "She had to have an emergency surgery."

"Emergency surgery?" My mind went through every possible scenario. What could have happened?

"Why don't you go talk to her. She's right in there." Kat motioned to the door beside us.

My fingers touched my bottom lip. I looked over at Scott and without another word, I pushed down on the handle and rushed into the room.

"Mom!" Mia shouted. Tears poured from her eyes the moment she saw me.

She reached her arms out toward me. Something she used to do when she was a child. "Oh, Mia, baby." I enveloped her into my arms, holding her tight. I never wanted to let her go. She was my baby girl and always would be. When she hurt, I hurt. I missed her so much. "Are you all right?"

Her lips and chin trembled as the tears streamed down her face. "I'm not okay," she whispered.

I sucked her back into my arms and held her while we both cried. Scott appeared moments later or maybe he had been there the whole time; I wasn't sure. My focus was on my daughter. She needed me more than ever. Actually, we needed each other.

"Hey," Scott said from the other side of the bed.

"Dad," Mia sobbed.

She went from my arms to his. I threw my arms around them both. We needed each other at this moment in time. From here on out, we were a family that helped one another. A family that leaned on each other. A family that talked about our problems, at least I hoped we would be after everything that had happened. Everything that had tried to tear us apart.

Fifty-Six

Mia

Mom stood looking around the room. I sat back against the pillow, the salty tears still leaking from my eyes.

"Kat wouldn't tell us what happened. She said to ask you," mom said, sitting back down on the bed, facing me.

Dad was on one side and her on the other. She handed me a few tissues.

"What happened at Kat's house?" Dad asked, pulling the chair to the side of the bed and sitting down.

My eyes moved from his face to hers. I wasn't ready to tell them but I knew they weren't leaving until I did. Besides, I didn't want the doctor to disclose the information. It was my place to break the sad news to them that they would never be grandparents.

"The doctor said I had some internal bleeding."

"Internal bleeding?" Mom questioned. "From what? How?"

I swallowed, staring down at the blanket laid upon me. "They call it maternal hemorrhage. Due to the miscarriage." I scanned their faces. They looked at one another, then back at me.

"Trevor?" Dad questioned.

I wished, I thought. "No, it was Ethan's." I swallowed the acidic bile entering the back of my throat.

Mom sucked in a breath, tears brimming in her eyes again.

"Ethan's?" Mom mouthed.

I nodded.

"I will kill that boy!"

"Dad!" I yelped.

"I'm sorry, but he deserves to pay for this. For what he did to you," dad replied. "God knows how many others there are."

"And he will. We will make sure he does," mom stated.

~

My dad left twenty minutes ago in search of coffee and snacks. It was just my mom and I in the room. That was a side of him I had never seen before, if ever. He was so angry.

"Mom?" I questioned.

"Yes, sweetie," she replied, squeezing my hand.

"I'm sorry that we won't be able to give you any grandchildren."

She shook her head. "Don't. You have no reason to be sorry. As long as I have you, that's all that matters."

Tears streamed down my face from her words. She leaned forward and took me in her arms again, cradling me as we rocked side-to-side. I opened my eyes when someone came into the room. I pulled away, looking around my mom.

"Aiden?" I questioned.

Mom turned around to see who I was talking to when she said. "Olivia?"

"Who's Olivia?" I asked.

"She's my new receptionist," mom replied, pointing toward Aiden in the doorway.

"No, that's Aiden. We met when I was in the hospital last month."

"It's actually Aiden. I wasn't sure what your mom knew about me, if anything at all, so I used a different name when I applied for the job," Aiden said.

"You work for my mom?" I asked.

"So, your name isn't Olivia?" mom asked, looking confused.

Aiden shook her head and walked toward the bed, standing where my dad had stood.

"How did you know I was in the hospital?" I asked.

"I volunteer here a couple days a week and saw your name on the board and... well, I was a little afraid you might have, umm, you know," Aiden said, twisting her finger around the locks of her hair. "It is how we met in the first place."

"Why would you lie to me?" mom asked, her eyes pinned on Aiden.

Aiden sat in the chair next to the bed. "I wanted to see what kind of person you were; not that I thought it was your fault for your sons' actions. I thought maybe if I could get to know you, I would eventually tell you what he did to me," Aiden stated, then continued, "Mia and I were in the same hospital last month. We became friends instantly. I knew who you were the whole time. We were in there for the same reasons."

"But you're, okay?" I asked. "I found you on the floor. There was so much blood."

"What?" Mom questioned.

Aiden looked from my mom to me before speaking. "Yeah, I uh, I found out I was pregnant."

I looked over at my mom. "I just lost my baby too," I replied. The next words out of her mouth made my insides stir, feeling sick to my stomach.

"I was raped by your brother, Ethan," Aiden said in a hushed voice. She turned to my mom. "By your son."

Fifty-Seven
Judith

I jolted to the restroom across the room. A sour bitter taste entered my mouth, burning my throat. I stood over the toilet, but nothing came out. My face flushed and I clutched a hand to my chest.

"Jud, is everything okay? Are you sick?" Scott asked from behind me. He moved his hand across my back in a circular motion.

"I'm fine," I lied, but he knew it was just what I said when I didn't want to tell him something.

He leaned forward, whispering in my ear. "Who's the girl?"

If I thought he was pissed off earlier, there was no telling what he was going to do once he found out about Aiden. "I think she should be the one to tell you who she is," I replied, rinsing out my mouth and spitting into the sink, trying to avoid eye contact with him.

We both walked back to the bed.

"Aiden," I swallowed. "This is Scott, my husband and Mia's father."

They both nodded, then Scott spoke. "Have I met you before? Are you from Mia's school?"

"No, I live in Lovell now," Aiden replied.

"Then how do you and Mia know each other?" Scott asked.

We all looked at one another before Aiden spoke. "Mia and I were at the same hospital last month. Scott, I'm not going to beat around the bush with you. I've held this in too long. When I met Mia in the hospital, I befriended her because I knew she was Ethan's sister." Aiden said, looking from Scott to Mia, who seemed shocked by her words.

"I had been watching her at the football games and even followed her home one night."

"How did you know Ethan was her brother?" I asked.

"He came to a game at my school. We were playing against Crawford. I spotted him talking to Mia," Aiden hesitated. "The only thought I had was to warn her. To keep her safe because I didn't want what happened to me to happen to her. I followed her and her boyfriend home after the game. I parked down the street, trying to find the courage to approach her, then that was when Ethan arrived and parked at the curb."

"I'm sorry, but what were you protecting her from?" Scott asked, looking at all of us.

I met Aiden's eyes and nodded.

"I was raped by your son Ethan and afterward, I tried to end my life. I met Mia at the hospital and then found out I was pregnant. It was Ethan's baby."

I watched Scott's mouth drop open. He stepped away from the bed. It only took a few minutes before the information sunk in. His face turned a dark red. He stared at her, his eyes drifting down before stopping. "I've seen that tattoo before. The half heart and semi-colon on your arm. He turned toward me. "The pictures. She's one of the girls in the photos."

He was right. I pulled out my cell phone and opened my photo app. I recalled taking pictures of the photos when I found them before deciding to keep them. I scanned through them until I landed on the one of Aiden. I handed my phone to her. "Is this you?"

Aiden nodded.

"Please look at the other pictures. Maybe there's someone else you may know in them."

~

When the police arrived at the hospital, Aiden told them everything. How she met Ethan and what happened. Then they asked Mia some of the same questions. Scott and I were beside ourselves. We had raised a horrible person, without even knowing what he was doing to these girls. It was awful to hear about what my son had done. What he was capable of. I didn't know that side of him. None of us did and I felt ashamed of him, and of myself.

One of the officers' guided Scott and I out into the hall.

"So, here's what will happen. Ethan has been arrested. He will be charged with two counts of rape, unless these other girls in the photos come forward and press charges, then the count rises. A search and seizure will be done of your home. If new evidence surfaces, he could be charged with more than the rape," Officer Wallace stated.

My head whooshed with dizziness. So much was happening, I couldn't process everything spinning inside my head. I placed my hand on the wall beside me for leverage. Scott must have been watching because he wrapped his arm around me to keep me from falling to the floor.

"Do whatever you have to do Officer Wallace. Our son needs to pay for everything he has done to these girls and their families," Scott said.

Officer Wallace placed a hand on Scott's shoulder. "I'm truly sorry you both are going through this, and I will do whatever I can to help you. I don't have any children myself, but if something like this were to have happened to my niece, I wouldn't stop until the person was behind bars."

"Thanks," I mumbled.

Officer Rifkin exited the room, stopping beside Officer Wallace. "Okay, I got both their statements. Are you ready to head back to the precinct?"

"Yeah, I'm finished here," Officer Wallace replied. "We'll be in touch."

We both nodded.

"I'm not sure I can take much more of this," I said.

"I know what you mean. I just wish I had known sooner. Maybe I could have stopped him from doing what he did or was doing."

"You can't blame yourself. We can't blame ourselves for this. We didn't know. How could we have known?" I replied.

"Now we make sure it never happens again," Scott said.

Epilogue

Mia

One Year Later

I took one last look in the mirror before running out the door. I had only been at UCLA for a month now.

"Hey, you ready?" Trevor asked, leaning against the wall outside my dorm room.

It sucks that we have to wait a year before we can live off campus. "Yeah," I replied. "I slept through my alarm, again. I was up late studying for this quiz Professor Greene sprung on us."

"But it's only the first week of school?" Trevor questioned.

"I know, right? He said this isn't high school anymore, so expect quizzes every week."

"Brutal. Any idea what you want to do tonight? Dinner, movie, anything you want."

"Anything?" I questioned, a smile spreading across my face. I had been wanting to go to this restaurant named Èlephante in Santa Monica.

He leaned over and kissed me, then flung his arm around my shoulder. We headed down the stairs to the outside. I gazed up at the sun. The heat warmed my face, making me feel at peace with myself. Something I hadn't felt in a long time. Even after my brother had been convicted for what he'd done, I still had nightmares. I had gone to therapy twice a week until a month ago when I moved to California with Trevor. Though my mom said if I feel the need to get a therapist out here, she will find one for me.

When it had come time to tell Trevor all the secrets I had kept from him, he was surprisingly supportive. He sat and listened to the things that were done to me. He cried when I said I wanted to die from what my brother did. Then the miscarriage. I knew Trevor loved me, but I hadn't known exactly how much. He had done nothing but console me and love me. Promising that nothing will ever happen like that again to me. He would make sure of that.

All around me, the sunlight glimmered off the windows of the building, causing a prism effect and refracting into mini rainbows. I especially liked the palm trees which reminded me of the Bahamas. At least the good parts. The way the top of the trees swayed in the breeze. It felt like paradise all over again.

As for my brother, Ethan, three other girls came forward once they heard Ethan had been arrested. There were six of us total, but the sixth girl had committed suicide a week after Ethan had assaulted her. My brother's trial took several months. After all testimonies were given, the judge sentenced him to life in prison with no chance of parole. He had six counts of rape and three deaths. The judge had included the deaths of Aiden's and my baby.

My brother will never see the light of day again outside of prison. I and the other girls can hopefully find a way to cope and live a healthy life with no fear of him coming after us. As I think about it, I know it will take a long time for us to heal. Rape can tear your life apart if you let it, which I almost had. What he had done to me can never be forgiven or forgotten, but I won't let him keep me from living my life. A happy, fulfilling life.

As for Aiden, she still works for my mom as her receptionist. We have gotten close after everything, and we talk every week on the phone. Aiden has decided to go to college and get her master's degree in Psychology. She would like to help other women who have been sexually assaulted.

As for my mom and me, we have become closer than we had ever been. We talk every day, even if only for a minute. I couldn't imagine my life without her beside me. As for my father, he was still angry at what my brother had done and still apologizes for his actions, even when it wasn't my father's fault. Ethan made a choice. Six bad choices and he will pay for what he has done to all of us.

I leaned into Trevor as we walked down the sidewalk toward our first classes. I honestly don't know what I'd do without him beside me. Trevor gave me a reason to live. A reason to still be here on this earth. For him and me to love one another until it was our time to go from this world. Not how I had tried to leave. Not by the result of what my brother did to me. But by God's choice.

They say, everything happens for a reason, whatever those reasons might be. But I'm not going to allow my brother to control my thoughts or how I live the rest of my life. I am stronger now and I have the support from my family, friends, and the love of my life. Don't let the circumstances that happen in your life to consume your life. You can overcome the battle just one day at a time.

Authors Note:

Suicide may seem like a way out for many people. I, myself, have dealt with the thoughts of suicide and have tried several times when I was a teenager. I struggled with not wanting to live because I didn't see a purpose; sometimes that's still an issue for me. I don't know where I fit in. Or who I can talk to without feeling judged for having such thoughts and feelings. Like it is something I can shut off and place on a shelf. Instead, I hide it away inside wishing and hoping it would just find the door and leave. I'm tired of the games my head plays, and I can't shut it off. Leaving me with myself to pretend I am absolutely fine and even that becomes hard for me to do.

There's so much sadness inside me then and now. I wanted to fit in with the kids at school but never felt good enough. I was bullied every day and back then it wasn't something the school seemed to care about. Today there are still issues with teen suicide and bullying. The teachers and faculty need to make this a priority. I didn't know who I could talk to back when I was young, in the 80's; the topic wasn't up for discussion. You couldn't openly talk about suicide or depression.

This book and many of my other novels/novellas are topics of bullying and suicide. Some deeper than others. I don't want people to feel discouraged after reading my books or that it will trigger my readers. I can't stop it or control what people do or think. It's just the way of life. We are all here for a certain purpose; we just don't know what that is yet. I keep searching when I know I just need to let things be and unfold as they come.

My daughter and best friend help me to deal with these emotions that try and control me. And I am truly grateful to have them in my life. There's a new thought process I'm using lately. Whenever something happens in your life that harms you or someone says mean things about you, don't let the situation or person get inside your head, instead drop it, leave it, and let it go. Walk away from the negative. Don't let it define who you are. There's a book titled, "Emptying out the Negative" by Joel Osteen. A must read for not just people struggling with the negative thoughts that are weighing us down, but for anyone that is lost and needs to find themselves. Leave the past behind you and move forward with positive thoughts. Drop it, Leave it, Let it go. Don't let our past define us. We are only here for a short time, so let's try and make it the greatest life we can live.

On an end note, if you're struggling with thoughts of suicide and deal with bullying at school or at work, just know you're not alone and that there are people out there that can help you. Your parents are there for some of you but if not try and find a friend or a teacher, someone you can open up to. Someone that will just listen without trying to fix you because in all honesty, no one can fix you but you…

How to handle a suicidal person?

Listen and take them seriously.

Accept what they're saying.

If they start talking, try not to interrupt or add your feelings to the conversation. It's not about you.

Let them know you care and are concerned for their well-being.

Just be there for them no matter what.

Let them know they are not alone.

Let them know that they can always contact you if they need someone to talk to.

- 988 Suicide and Crisis Lifeline
- Call the Lifeline at 800-273-8255, 24 hours a day, 7 days a week.

Acknowledgements

Here's where I get to say thank you to all the people that mean so much to me and helped make my dream as a published author come true. First and foremost, I want to thank my readers for reading my books. I don't know what I'd do without your support. Thank you for everything.

I want to thank my family and friends for all the support and encouragement they give me with every story I write. Thank you, and I love you all so much!

About the Author

Donna M. Zadunajsky started out writing children's books before she accomplished and published her first novel, *Broken Promises*, in June 2012. She since has written several more novels and her first novella, *HELP ME!* Book 1 in the series, which is about teen suicide and bullying.

Milton Keynes UK
Ingram Content Group UK Ltd.
UKHW040257291024
450401UK00015B/226/J